CLOSURE

ERICK WILLIAMS

This a work of fiction. Any resemblance to actual persons living or dead references to real people, events songs, business establishments or locales is purely coincidental. All characters are fictional all events are imaginative.

No part of this publication may be reproduced, transmitted in any form or by any means electronic mechanical, photocopying, recording or otherwise without the written permission of the author.

TABLE OF CONTENTS

The Recap 4

1 Dez and Jackson 6

2 Monday morning, KJ and Ericka 16

3 Vicky and KJ are walking 23

4 Vicky's been in the kitchen 30

5 Vicky's BOTH EXCITED AND NERVOUS 36

6 As she is walking towards Dez 43

7 Omar driving 50

8 Vicky's Phone pings she has 55

9 Vicky shocked that Keith's on the 64

10 As Omar Backs his truck into 69

11 The female officer pushes a button for 74

12 Vicky's sitting on her bed 81

13 "Well if there are not any more 88

14 Vicky, KJ, and Ericka are at the 95

15 The door is shut she 99

16 She goes back to the couch 104

17 Antonio observes Kj sitting with 110

18 That night KJ's reading in the kitchen 115

19 As she drives home 123

20 Christmas Day!! Vicky and 128

21 Omar and Dez arrive at 132

22 The holiday season is over 138

23 Vicky shows her phone 145

24 Later that night at 9 pm 150

25 The horn sounds over the loudspeaker 158

26 Vicky's cell phone Alarm is Beeping 167

27 Vicky texts Back, ... 173

28 "what do you want to know?" 180

29 Friday afternoon KJ and Ericka 186

30 Omar limps to Dezera's 190

Acknowledgments 210

THE RECAP

KJ'S AT THE basketball court, he reaches inside his jacket pocket and pulls out the gun. Vicky screams, "Oh my God he is going to shoot them, boys!"

Antonio pulls up to the right side of Tristan's car, Tristan looks over at them with fear in his eyes, and without saying anything, he starts his car backs up then drives away. Both Vicky and Antonio get out of the car, she yells back to Dre and Ericka, "Stay in the car!"

Antonio walking to the court yells," KJ!"

KJ caught off guard turns around and looks at Antonio, with his voice quivering, "I need to do this for Jordan." He then turns back around and points the gun at Dez.

Antonio walks slowly towards him and responds with "No you don't. You think Jordan wants you to do this?"

Vicky catches up with Antonio tells KJ, "Please son put the gun down, this is not the way."

Still pointing the gun at Dez, says with tears in his eyes, "I'm tired of being afraid."

Vicky her voice trembling with emotion, "It's your brother's birthday and I got fired today, I was torn up inside, then Antonio calls and tells me that you are missing. I was scared you were dead, I was lost to the point I was going to kill myself, Ericka coming home from school was the reason I didn't. She saved me and didn't even know it."

KJ shocked by what he just heard turns around and looks at his mother asks, "You were going to kill yourself?"

When KJ turns away, Dre, Jackson, and the other dude see this as their chance and take off running.

Vicky's eyes fully teared up answers, "Yeah, Ericka coming home happy made me realize I have a reason to live,.. actually 2 reasons," she's smiling as she says it.

She continues, "You were the last person to talk to your brother you promised him that you would not get caught up in this. Keep your promise to him. Give me the gun."

KJ places the gun in Vicky's hand, she then gives it to Antonio as he approaches from behind. He drops the magazine racks it back and realizes that there wasn't a round chambered. "Did you know that the gun wasn't loaded?"

"What are you talking about?"

"There wasn't a bullet in the chamber. You think he was setting you up?" Antonio asks.

1

DEZ AND JACKSON are sitting in Dez's living room still shaken up from the encounter with KJ.

Jackson plops down on the couch, Dez with nervous energy paces back and forth in front of him still pissed about the exchange.

"Can you believe that nigga drew down on us?" Dez asks in a loud aggressive voice.

Jackson responds, "You think that fool was going to smoke us?"

Dez stops pacing looks at Jackson responds, "You packing. Why didn't you smoke him?"

"I don't got it with me. We balling, I wasn't giving that fool no thought. Jackson pauses for a moment then drops his head, for a second he looks back at Dez and asks, "You wanted me to smoke him in front of his mom? Come on bro even you can't be that cold."

Dez looks back at him rationalizes, "It's either us or him, he drew on us first we just defending ourselves."

Heavy steps are coming down the hall, towards the living room, both Dez and Jackson get quiet and look n the direction the footsteps are coming from.

Out steps a heavy dark-skinned man about 6'0" with a large potbelly a scraggly full beard and a nappy old school afro. He has on some white boxers and a white t-shirt and a white t-shirt and a gray cotton bathrobe, it's Omar Dez's father.

He stares at Jackson in and a low monotone voice tells him, "You need to leave."

Jackson feeling the intensity in his voice, gets up without saying a word gives Dez the head nod as he walks by him.

After Jackson is gone Dez looks at him and asks, "What's up pops?"

Omar walks over to a dark brown leather recliner and sits down. He pulls out a pack of cigarettes from his robe and lights one up, in the same tone he tells Dez, "Sit down we need to talk."

Antonio is driving with Vicky in the front passenger seat, KJ, Ericka, and Dre are all in the backseat. Vicky turns around and yells at KJ "What the hell is wrong with you?" You get a gun and going to shoot that boy. You really are trying to end up like your brother…. dead!"

Antonio driving in a calmer voice, "Relax baby sis, this is not the place to talk about this. Do you still want to go see Jordan?"

Vicky all unnerved and agitated sighs deeply and answers, "No let's just go home," with a sarcastic tone adds, "Well maybe we should since this is where KJ is going to end up."

 KJ in a frustrated tone responds, "Can you just drop it?"

Vicky turns around again in a loud voice, "You get a gun and are about to kill a boy and I'm supposed to act like nothing happened."

Antonio in a louder angrier voice, "Look we said this wasn't the right time to talk about it. Where did you get a gun from?"

He looks back at KJ with the car rear view mirror, KJ turns away looks out the window.

Vicky turns around and pops him on the leg, "What? You're not going to answer?" He continues to stare out the window ignoring her.

Antonio, "It was that knucklehead, that drove off when we pulled up wasn't it."

KJ glances at him without saying anything.

"I knew it. I'm take care of the gun for you."

"What are you going to do? Take it to the police?" He asked nervously.

"I should, but there would be too many questions. Trust me nobody will find it."

They all quiet down after a few seconds he looks in the rearview mirror at Dre, "You need to tell me how to get to your house." Dre shakes his head accordingly.

Ericka asks the question on everybody's mind, "Were you going to really shoot him?"

Dez's sitting on the couch he leans back asks, "What's up? Why you make Jackson leave?"

Omar sits up in the recliner, leans in, and looks at Dez, "I heard you and Jackson talking."

"What are you talking about?" Dez asks feigning innocence.

"Don't play stupid games with me," he answers back in an annoyed tone continues, "Loud as y'all were talking I couldn't help but hear you, now tell me what happened."

Dez replies, "I didn't know you were home," he pauses and takes a deep breath, "Me Jackson and Brent were at the courts and this fool came out of nowhere he doesn't say nothing, and pulls a gun and points it at me."

"Then what happened?"

"His mom and dad showed up and started talking to him. When he turned around, we saw our chance and took off."

"Do you know this boy?"

Dez answers in an excited voice, "That fool that DJ smoked, it's his little brother."

Omar hears this and drops back into the recliner sighs very deeply. His mind is racing thinking about how the cycle of violence is repeating itself.

"Y'all were talking and it sounds like you were planning on doing something" he pauses in a deeper louder tone "DON'T!"

Dez not happy hearing this comes back with, "What am I supposed to do let some nigga draw down on me and not do anything about it? You got me fucked up!"

Omar hears this he jumps out of the recliner steps over the coffee table snatches Dez up by his shirt and yells at him, "You got me fucked up, if you think you can talk like that to me in my house boy. I'm still your father and I will snatch your heart out if you disrespect me like that again!"

He pushes Dez back on the couch and limps to the kitchen.

Dez breathing hard and angry sits on the couch as tears well up in his eyes, yells, "So what would you have done? If this nigga came at you back in the day?"

He stops and looks back at Dez, "When I was running with the 169 boys, we would have caught him in a dark alley and beat him so bad his mother wouldn't even recognize him. That's why I did over 10 years in the pen. Your brother has 30 plus years before he can even see parole. At some point, we need to end the cycle of everybody in this family going to prison. I'm your father I don't want you to make the same mistakes I did, I failed with DJ, but I won't fail with you no matter how hard you push me."

Dez's hearing but not listening asks, "What if he comes at me again?"

Omar pauses for a second thinks about the question, "I will reach out and talk to his parents to see if we can come to some kind of agreement before someone else gets killed."

Antonio pulls up into the driveway and parks behind Vicky's red Camry. Ericka and KJ are in the back seat both have their headphones on. Ericka opens the back car door yells "Bye Uncle Antonio, see you later." He answers, "Come here and give me a hug." She goes up to the driver's side door and hugs him.

KJ gets out without saying a word and walks into the house.

Vicky yells out, "I need to talk with your Uncle for a few minutes, I will be in to get dinner going."

Vicky looks at Antonio, with an irritated tone states, "This has been one of the worst days of my life. I got fired, was close to killing myself, and then KJ almost kills a boy." She puts her head down and shakes it slowly taking deep long breaths.

Antonio startled by her comment asks, "So what's this about you were going to kill yourself?"

She lifts up her head and answers, "In a moment of weakness, I thought about suicide, Ericka coming home from school snapped me out of it."

"So, this happened before I came over. Why didn't you say something?"

In an agitated tone, she answers, "What was I supposed to say? 'I almost committed suicide today?' I was so worried about KJ I didn't have time to think about myself."

Antonio in a more relaxed tone, "Relax baby sis, I'm on your side. I was just asking out of concern. So, you good now?"

Vicky really uncomfortable talking about it, responds, "If you're asking if I'm thinking about doing it, no I'm good. Right now, I need to get KJ straight."

"About that, you need to go easy with him he is in a fragile state and you don't want to push him. Give him a little space, I will talk with him later when things have cooled down."

"Okay, I will let you deal with it. He seems to be bonding with you."

Antonio in a calm voice, "Look I got you if you need anything just let me know."

She looks at him and smiles, "Alright remember you said that."

He smiles back at her, "No problem."

In his room KJ is laying down on his bed his mind racing, thinks back to holding the gun in his hand and the power he felt even if it was just for a few seconds.

I should have shot him when I had the chance, he thinks continuing, *what was mom talking about she was going to kill herself? Was she lying to distract me so I wouldn't shoot him? Then Uncle Antonio says the gun wasn't loaded, that Tristan was setting me up. I don't know what the fuck is going on.*

He sits up on the bed grabs his cell phone, texts Tristan,

Were you trying to set me up? He put his phone on the bed.

He turns over and sees the PS4 controller grabs it and turns on the system. Call of Duty is loading up, he sits up and gets ready to play the game.

His phone pings, he picks it up it's a text from Tristan "*Fool what you talking bout?*

He texts back, *Nigga you knew that shit wasn't loaded*

Tristan "Bro, I wasn't trying to set you up, I forgot to rack it back. Did you do it?

KJ Hell no! My mom and Uncle showed up, you think I can pop him in front of my mom.

Tristan Where's the piece?

KJ My uncle's got it. He says he is going to take care of it.

Tristan Bro there is something you need to know about the gun

KJ hears the door open as his mother comes into the house. She's walking towards his room. He puts his phone down and he takes a deep breath to prepare himself for the storm that is coming his way.

She knocks on the door and opens it up before he has a chance to respond. She leans in the room, KJ blurts out, "Mom I know you…. She cuts him off, "Look I didn't come in here to talk about what happened, I'm giving you some space, I think we both have some things that we are going through. Antonio told me he will get with you in a few days to make sure you are still good. I just wanted you to know I still love you and we will get through this."

He looks at her surprised not knowing exactly how to respond, "Ummm ok... thanks." She shuts the door walking away she yells,

"I'm ordering a pizza for dinner I really don't feel like cooking. I'll be in the living room waiting on the pizza. Oh, yeah, I got a text from Mr. White you have an appointment Monday. He yells back, "Okay."

KJ looks back at the tv and sees a message from "Dre-754 it reads," *We good bro?*

He ignores it and starts playing, after 15 minutes of playing his phone pings

It's a text from Storm, *What's up*

Playing Call of Duty, he answers.

Storm *Dre told me about what happened at the court*

KJ *It figures he does like to snitch.*

Storm *What are you talking about?*

KJ He *snitched on me to my mom.*

Storm *He probably saved you from doing something really stupid.*

KJ Yeah *whatever.*

Storm texts, *Y'all been boys too long to let this come between you.*

He reads the text stares at it for about 30, 40 seconds, finally puts the phone down on his stand next to the PS controller just as he is about to pick up the controller his phone rings.

He picks it up, it's Dre.

Dre *in an aggressive angry tone, "Yo bro what's your problem?"*

KJ, *"You snitched on me."*

Dre," *Fool you outta be thanking me, I probably saved your life. Do you really think you can kill somebody? This ain't some movie or game this here is real life."*

KJ *"Nigga you don't think I know that. All I was doing is getting payback for Jordan."*

Dre, *"Aight bro if that's how you see it. I'm tired of always saving your ass anyway. Later for you fool."*

KJ hangs up.

2

MONDAY MORNING, KJ AND ERICKA

are at the breakfast table eating cereal. He is both nervous and anxious, this is the first day back in his normal classes. He doesn't know what is going around about the deal at the basketball court.

Vicky comes into the kitchen wearing her robe and slippers.

Ericka looks at her and asks, "You're not going to work today?"

"I told y'all I got fired."

KJ "So what happened? Why did you get fired?"

She stands there silently at the sink, not sure if she wants to go into the whole situation about what happened fearing it might lead to a bunch of questions, that she doesn't want to answer.

"I got caught up in my feelings and let a racist, get under my skin. I should have been smarter."

KJ and Ericka look at each other even more confused than before, Vicky notices this, and says louder, "It's a lot to explain. Just finish your breakfast." She looks at KJ, "Please don't talk about what happened Friday."

Ericka, "It's already online."

"There isn't nothing we can do about what other people say, just how we respond to it." As she is saying this she realizes the irony in her statement she chuckles to herself and shakes her head thinks *if I would have had that attitude Friday I would still have a job.*

"Okay let's finish up, we have to get going." Ericka standing up asks, "So what if somebody says something to me about it?"

Vicky replies, "Just don't answer them, ignore it, say you don't know what they are talking about."

She looks at KJ and tells him directly emphasizing, "You definitely don't talk about it at school. You have a meeting with your probation officer after school and we don't need anything getting back to him about this."

Ericka, walks to her room, "So you want him to lie? You told us we should never lie."

Vicky annoyed about Ericka's persistence on the subject responds, "Sometimes it is necessary to lie to protect the ones you love, and I will lie, cheat, steal and even kill to protect y'all that's my duty as your mom."

Vicky drops Ericka off at Zoey so they can walk to school together, she drives K to school. She wants to talk with him to emphasize that he does not discuss the incident.

"I will be here to pick you up after school so we can meet with your probation officer. If anything happens today, I will be at home on the computer looking for a job.

 KJ anxiously answers, "Okay mom I got it don't talk about it," he opens the car door, "See you after school." He gets out and jogs to the building. Vicky watches him go into the building she is worried about what might happen

Back home Vicky goes into her room grabs her laptop comes back into the living room sits on the couch. She flips open the computer, then it hits her, the whole process of looking for a job, updating her resume, sending it out, getting tons of rejection. Hopefully, get an interview or two. She sits back on the couch, thinks, *no use in getting frustrated before I even get started.* She sits back up and opens her documents folder and realizes she doesn't even have a resume on the computer. She flops back on the couch, says out loud to no one "I'm really not in the mood to do this, she sits for what seems like an eternity but is actually two minutes gets up, and gets her phone from her room. Talking to herself once again, "I need to call Dr. Murvin." She finds her number in her contacts goes through automated phone prompts she finally hears a real female voice.

Receptionist, *"Good morning Dr. Murvin's office. How can I help you?"*

Vicky, *"Yes I would like to schedule an appointment to see Dr. Murvin as soon as possible."*

"Is there some kind of emergency going on?"

"Well, I had a situation this past weekend where I was thinking about committing suicide?"

The receptionist excitedly asks *"Are you in the hospital? Are you hurt?"*

Vicky in a calm voice, *"No I'm at home I'm not injured I just would like to talk to Dr. Murvin about it. Get some things off my chest."*

The receptionist typing on the computer, *"Right now she doesn't have any openings for the next two weeks."*

"I was hoping to get in sometime this week."

"I will let you know if anything opens up. Is there a certain time that works best for you?"

"Anytime is good, I'm unemployed at the present moment."

"I'm sorry to hear that."

"Thank you," Vicky attempting to keep a positive attitude responds, "They say God doesn't give you more than you can bear, when a door closes a window opens."

"Good to hear that you haven't quit. Look I will make sure you see, Dr. Murvin this week even if it's on her lunch hour."

"Thank you, sis, I appreciate your help. Just give me a call when you have an opening. Have a good day."

"You too, bye." She hangs up.

Vicky hangs up and puts the phone by her computer. She stares at her computer, dreading what she has to do. Knowing she has no choice she takes a deep breath opens it up and gets to work.

Vicky is out front of the school waiting for KJ to come out. She arrived early, just to make sure she is not late taking him to his appointment. She hears the school buzzer ring at three, all of a sudden, the doors burst open and a mass of humanity leaves the building. Sitting in her car, peering out of the passenger window searching for KJ. She sees Dre as he is talking with a girl walking towards the bus. He does not notice her, she continues looking for KJ after another 5 minutes as the crowd is thinning out KJ walks out by himself. She spots him and blows her horn to get his attention after blowing three to four times, he looks up and walks over to the car, he puts his backpack in the back and jumps in the front.

She starts the car and drives off curious about his first day asks, "So how was it?"

KJ in a low mellow tone replies, "Cool nothing special."

Trying to get him to engage in a conversation, "I saw Dre walking to the bus talking to a girl. Is that his girlfriend?"

His face immediately turns sour she notices this, "Is something wrong?"

"It's nothing I just don't feel like talking about him."

"Okay, whatever, when we get here don't say anything about Friday."

He answers back irritated, "Okay I get it you don't have to keep saying it over and over." The car is quiet the rest of the ride.

As they make the left turn into the Allen County Juvenile Detention he says, "I wish Uncle Antonio could be here."

Vicky turns into a parking spot sensing his nervousness, "I texted him he says he couldn't make it."

She parks the car they both get out and walk into the lobby of the Detention Center. He looks up at the clock it's 3:45, he walks in and takes a seat in an orange vinyl chair directly under the clock. Vicky walks to the reception desk it is enclosed behind a sliding plastic glass barrier. The receptionist slides the glass to the side as she steps up to the counter.

"How may I help you?"

"I'm Mrs. Skyy and my son KJ has an appointment, with Mr. White at 4."

The receptionist replies, "Oh I'm sorry Mr. White left early today, he wasn't feeling well."

KJ slumping in the chair hears this and sits up he's relieved a smile creeps over his face. There is no chance he has to talk about Friday, so he is good.

Vicky has mixed emotions, she's happy about the fact that KJ won't have a meeting today, a little miffed that no one contacted her about rescheduling the meeting.

"Well somebody could have called me to let me know, so I wouldn't have wasted my time?"

She answers back in an apologetic tone, "I'm sorry Mrs. Skyy, I don't have a copy of Mr. White's schedule, he wasn't feeling too well when he left maybe he forgot."

Vicky gives her a displeased look and mumbles, "Whatever," she turns around and tells KJ, "Let's go."

He excitedly jumps out of the chair and they walk out, as they walk on the sidewalk KJ's excitement changes quickly as he sees Dez and his father walking towards them.

3

VICKY AND KJ ARE WALKING straight towards Omar and Dez. She doesn't know who they are. KJ sees Dez walking towards him and he tenses up. Dez glares at KJ not looking away for a second, he mumbles, "That's the nigga that almost smoked me."

Omar hears this and with his right-hand points at KJ, "Who him?"

Dez answers back angrily, "Yeah!"

Vicky still unaware of the scene unfolding in front of her turns to the right and is walking through the parking lot to the car.

Omar sees this and calls out to her, "Excuse me, Miss, can I talk to you for a minute?"

She's caught off guard by the question stops between two cars looks at him and responds, "Excuse me?"

He does a slow shuffle/limp towards her.

Her guard is up as he approaches, she cautiously asks, "What's up?"

After about a twenty-yard jog he is winded, and he takes a few seconds to catch his breath. He introduces himself, "I'm Omar Russell, I'm Dez's father."

He looks back and sees Dez and KJ inches away from each other staring one another down.

Dez snarls, "What's good?"

"Whatchu tryna do?" KJ snarls back as he is pulling up his pants.

Omar and Vicky hear them mouthing back and forth. Omar yells, "Dez!! Dez!! Get over here right now!"

Dez looks at him and then stares back at KJ once more, "I'll catch you around," then turns and walks to his father.

Vicky with her right hand waves KJ to come over to her.

As Dez walks over to him, Omar in an angry tone asks, "How stupid are you, boy? Getting into a fight in front of juvenile probation. You just trying to get locked up." Dez is not paying attention he continues to glare at KJ.

KJ walks up to Vicky still eyeballing Dez slowly shakes his head and asks "Can I get the keys? I'll wait in the car." She reaches into her shoulder pack gives him the keys. He grabs them and walks to the car.

Omar looks back at Vicky and tells her, "I'm sorry about that, I heard about what happened on the court between our boys."

As she is listening to him she tenses up, she doesn't know where he is going with this.

He continues, "I was hoping we could meet to talk about it."

Still unsure, she answers, "What do we need to talk about?"

He senses her uneasiness, answers, "I wanted to talk so hopefully, we can avoid any more killing."

Vicky relaxes somewhat after she hears this, "Okay sure I would like that. When can we meet?"

He grabs his phone off his belt clip and checks the time, "Right now I have to meet with his probation officer, then I need to get to work."

He gives her his phone, "Here put your number and I will text you to set something up."

She is a little uncomfortable about giving her phone number, but she thinks, *I need to try if he is willing to.* She puts her number in and gives it back to him.

He grabs his phone and starts texting, "I'm sending you a quick text so you can have my number."

Her phone dings in her shoulder pack.

He hears the phone ding, "Great!! Well, we need to get in here for this appointment, I will be reaching out in the next week or so."

"Okay." She walks to her car where KJ is in the front seat leaning back, with his earbuds in. He sits up when he hears the car door open,

He asks, "Well what did he say?"

She is not sure if she should tell him she coolly replies, "Not much, we were just talking."

In the juvenile detention lobby, Omar and Dez are sitting in the lobby, Dez's sitting in the same chair that KJ was in earlier. Omar sitting to the right whispers, "What's up with you? Fighting in front of the probation department? The last thing you need is to get into a fight in front of your probation officer."

"I'm sorry pops, I wasn't even thinking about it, but I can't have fools thinking I'm soft, he drew down on me and he is still breathing, that doesn't sit right with me."

Omar's frustrated hearing him talk like this replies, "Boy DJ killed his brother in front of him. How would you feel if you saw someone kill DJ? Wouldn't you want payback?"

Dez angrily answers, "Hell yeah and I'd get it too."

He looks at him shaking his head, "You need to change how you think. I already got one son in prison for murder, lost to the system. I don't want to lose you. If you keep thinking like that you are either going to end up in prison or the cemetery."

He changes the subject, "Before we go in here, don't say anything about what happened Friday."

Dez, surprised? "Why not, that fool pulled the gun on me, he was wrong."

Omar in a hushed tone answers, "Haven't we caused them enough pain? We are going to work this out between us, there ain't no reason to get these people involved."

Dez is frustrated and a little angry he feels like KJ punked him and is getting away with it. He believes his dad doesn't have his back.

They sit there quietly lost in their thoughts. After five minutes, the lobby door opens directly to the left. Mrs. Helen Brothers is his probation officer. Leaning through the door, she looks at them and in a cheerful voice asks, "Y'all ready to come back?"

They both look at each other and stand up together, Omar answers, "Sure let's do it."

Inside Mrs. Brother's office, they both sit down in two brown leather chairs that face her desk. Sitting behind her desk she looks at Dez and asks in a cheerful voice, "How's it going Dez?"

Dez looks over at his dad, then back at her replies, "It's alright I guess."

She notices the suspicious behavior and asks, "Is there something going on I should know?"

Omar quickly answers before Dez gets a chance, "On our way in he ran into that boy he got into a fight with at the basketball game."

Mrs. Brother's eyebrows raise with surprise, "What's his name I don't know him."

"KJ."

"Did anything happen?" she asks.

Dez shakes his head no, "That punk just runs his mouth too much" he mumbles.

She folds her hands in front of her and leans on her desk. Her tone is very serious she warns him, "You need to be careful, you are hanging by a thread, any little violation can get you locked back up and in court."

Dez nonchalantly mumbles, "Whatever."

Omar frustrated by his attitude, interjects, "Boy when are you going to start taking this serious? Your brother is doing time. Is that what you want?"

Mrs. Brothers stands up behind her desk puts her hands out, yells, "Truce, Truce, this is not the place, we don't need any family arguments." She sits back down and in a calmer voice asks, "Is there anything else going on that I need to know about?"

"No."

She pulls out a sheet of paper from a folder and looks at it, puts it down. "According to this report, you have missed fourteen days of school in the last month. Is this true?"

Once again, he nonchalantly answers, "I don't know, yea sure whatever."

His attitude pushes her final button, she stands up once again puts her hands on her desk, and leans in towards him, "I'm not going to play with you anymore. Any future reports of you violating your probation and I will have you picked up, I can't care more about your life than you do."

Omar to Mrs. Roberts, "My work schedule prevents me from getting him to school, but I'm telling you I will make sure he will be there, even if I have to switch shifts, please give him another chance."

She hears the desperation in his voice, and in a softer voice looks at Dez tells him, "Okay but don't forget what I said because I meant it."

Omar pulls his phone off his belt clip, looks at it, "I got to be at work in an hour. Is there anything else?"

She takes a deep breath, "No problem I think we covered everything. Just remember your probation fees are due in your next visit and you have a urinalysis coming up soon."

They all walk out, Dez walks ahead straight out of the building. Omar tells Mrs. Brothers, "No problem, see you next time. She waves bye as he walks out of the building.

Dez's standing at Omar's gray F150 truck with his back turned, Omar hits the clicker to unlock it and he gets in. Omar gets in before he starts the car asks, "What's your problem?"

"I wish you would have let me drop a dime on KJ. His ass would be getting arrested right now."

Omar starts the truck, "We talked about that already, let it go we can take care of this. I' don't have time right now but I'm going to text her later this week to set up the meeting, so y'all can bury this beef and be done with it."

4

VICKY'S BEEN IN THE KITCHEN the last two and a half hours in front of her laptop. It's been a week and she has been posting her resume relentlessly. She aimlessly scrolls through Ineed.com, frustrated that she has not even got a nibble on a job lead.

She looks up from the computer and stares out the window and takes a deep breath, she looks back down and grabs her cell phone, and texts Shea *What you doing?*

Ten minutes later, her phone dings with a text from Shea, *Finishing my work out what's up?*

Vicky texts, *Nothing much just here at the house job hunting.*

Shea, *You wanna do lunch? My treat.*

Of course, I never turn down a free meal LOL. What you thinking?

Shea, *What about McAlister's Deli?*

Vicky, *I've never been but I will give it a try.*

Shea, *Great I can meet you there in 20 minutes.*

Vicky *See you then.*

She saves her work and closes her laptop.

She arrives at the restaurant and the parking lot is full of the workday lunch crowd. She drives around the lot and does not see Shea, she drives to the back and parks She texts, Shea *I'm here parked in the back*

As she is putting her phone in her purse, Shea's white BMW x5 pulls up beside her to the left.

Shea steps out still wearing her red Adidas leggings with matching red yoga top, looking like she should be in one of those workout commercials you see on tv. Vicky's wearing blue jeans and a light blue t-shirt that says "Let it be." She feels self-conscious about her outfit once she sees Shea.

"How do you look so good even after working out?" she asks.

Shea laughs, "That's the whole point of working out. "Let's go.'"

There is a long line, after a ten-minute wait in the line. They place their order and take a seat in the back. Their order will be bought to their table.

Shea asks, "Girl how you doing?"

Vicky takes a deep breath and answers back in a somber voice, "It's been a crazy last few days. Between KJ's attitude and the job situation, I just needed a little bit of me-time."

 "I get it girl. We all do that's what working out does for me it recharges my battery. Maybe you outta come to the gym with me it couldn't hurt. I know the owner he would give you a great discount."

Vicky laughs at the inside joke. She replies "I don't know maybe. I haven't worked out in years, I would feel guilty working out when I should be job hunting." She switches gears, "Did I tell you that I ran into the father of Jordan's killer earlier this week?"

Shea surprised, "So what happened?"

"Well we were leaving from the probation department and they just happened to be coming in. I did not know who they were until KJ and that boy almost got into another fight right in front of the probation department. The boy's father then asked could he speak to me?"

"What did he say to you?"

"He asked if we could meet to talk about this ongoing beef between our kids."

Shea on the edge of her seat, "What did you tell him?"

Their food is brought to the table. Vicky stops talking she doesn't want their conversation to be overheard.

After the server leaves, Vicky continues, "Well I gave him my phone number so he could text me when he gets the chance."

Shea takes a bite of her turkey sandwich asks, "So has he?"

Vicky chewing her Italian sub sandwich swallows and answers, "No I 'm not sure he even will. Hopefully, he does this needs to come to an end."

Shea sipping on her tea answers, "Give him a few more days and see what happens."

"I will it seems he's got a pretty busy schedule."

Shea sandwich in hand says "Keep me posted." She takes another bite, looks up, and asks cautiously, "So how are you doing financially? You Okay?"

Vicky looks at her, in a low tone answers, "I can cover the bills for this month, between what I have in the bank and my last paycheck, after that, I don't know."

"I'm sure you will have something by then, but if you don't me and Antonio are here for you."

"Are you talking about a loan?"

"Sure, if you absolutely needed one."

She stares blankly at Shea not so much at her as through her, suggest, "What about a job instead of a loan?"

Surprised by the suggestion, she asks, "What would you do?"

"I don't know..... filing paperwork, answering phones, wiping down machines, I guess a combination between a receptionist and a janitor."

"You wouldn't mind doing that kind of work?"

"I'd feel better about myself knowing I earned a paycheck instead of taking a loan I would have to pay back."

Shea shakes her head, approvingly, "I can talk to your brother about it, he should be good with it."

Vicky tells her, "This would be temporary until I get on my feet."

Shea drinking her tea, says, "Understood." She looks at Vicky, unsure if she should bring up the next thing on her mind.

She swallows hard, and states, "I don't know how to bring this up so I'm just going to say it, Antonio mentioned that you were thinking about committing suicide. You want to talk about?"

She is still not completely comfortable talking about it, but it's easier talking about it with Shea than Antonio.

"I don't know exactly where to begin it just felt like the pressure of the world was on my back, I'm still dealing with Jordan's death, then getting fired on his birthday. KJ not answering his phone, my mind just went to a dark place. It felt like everything was falling apart around me all at the same time."

"So how come you didn't call me?" Shea asks.

She simply answers, "I don't know. I just wanted the pain to stop right then and there."

"So how are you feeling today?"

"I'm doing better I'm waiting to hear back from my Dr for an appointment. Hopefully, she will give me some pills to deal with my nerves."

Shea smiles and says, "Yeah pills are good." She looks her in the eyes reaches across the table and holds her hands, in a calm voice says, "You have too much to live for queen, everything you are going through right now, is short-term. I know you may not think that right now, especially with KJ acting out, but this is a phase, he is lost and confused but as long as you stay strong and true he will come through it fine. I know you've noticed he and Antonio are forming a bond. He is not going to let KJ fail, trust me on that." This time next year you will look back on this and laugh when you see how far you've come."

Vicky almost close to tears, tells her, "Thanks girl I needed that."

She gets a ping on her phone, pulls it out of her purse, reads it is a text, *"Hello I'm Sunny Givens with St. Anthony's Medical Center Human Resource, and we have received your application for the registered nurse position if you are still interested contact me at 570-230-1264 or email me at SunnyG@St. Anthony.com.*

Vicky excitedly jumps up, "Yes! Finally, things are going my way."

Shea jumps up too, "See! I told you things are about to change."

"Let me go girl, and get somewhere quiet to make this phone call."

"Alright go get that job, keep me posted." They hug and Vicky walks to her car. She hasn't been this happy in weeks.

5

VICKY'S BOTH EXCITED AND NERVOUS at the same time, she sits down on the couch anxious to call Mrs. Givens.

She inhales a really deep breath holds it for a few seconds exhales and dials the number.

On the fourth ring a female voice on the other answers, *"Good afternoon this is Mrs. Givens with St. Andrews Human Resources."*

"Yes, I'm Vicky Skyy and I received a text concerning the position of a registered nurse and I'm calling to let you know I'm interested."

Mrs. Givens is walking into the hospital lobby, replies *"You kind of caught me at an awkward time, I just returned from lunch and haven't made it to my office yet."*

Vicky leaning back on the couch, *"Well do you need me to call back?"*

"No, I got you on the phone, just bear with me for a few minutes," she says as she is getting on the elevator.

She continues *"Here is a little bit about the job, it's in the ED it has the standard staggered 12-hour shifts, you have to be available for holidays and weekends. The hourly* wage starts at 30 per hour and can increase depending on your experience. There's the opportunity for overtime, bonuses are offered. We have the full benefits package, medical, dental, and vision. If you are looking to further your education we offer tuition reimbursement."

Vicky likes what she hears, *"I have a few questions?"*

Mrs. Givens stepping off the elevator walks down the hall, *"I'm not sure if I will be able to answer them but go ahead shoot."*

Vicky asks, *"Well I just wanted to know what type of patient population do you serve and how many patients do you see a day?"*

"You will have to ask the nursing director, I do not have that information available to me at this time. We are doing interviews next week Monday through Friday from 9 to 4. What day and time is good for you."

Vicky pauses for a few seconds thinking she wants to get their early answers *"Tuesday at 10."*

Mrs. Givens in her office sitting at her desks logs on, *"I got you down at 10 Tuesday. Make sure you bring in your certifications."*

"Okay, I will see you then goodbye."

She hangs up.

On cue Ericka walks into the house, sees her mom sitting on the couch, and runs over and hugs her, this is the icing on Vicky's day.

"What's up mom?" Ericka asks.

"I got great news, I got a job interview on Tuesday."

"Great!"

"I haven't gotten it yet so I don't want to be too excited", she says trying to contain her emotions. She then turns towards Ericka "So how was school?"

Ericka gets up and starts walking to her room answers, "It was good. Zoey and Reign are going to see Space Slam today and asked if I could go?"

Vicky's excitement quickly turns, sour, "I'm sorry baby, with me not working, we don't have any extra money for movies right now."

"I already texted her and told her I could."

Vicky irritated that Ericka would be so presumptuous, "Why would you do that without asking first?"

The doorbell unexpectedly rings, Ericka runs to get it to stop the upcoming argument. Reign and Zoey are at the door, she quickly lets them in.

Vicky is happy to see Reign she doesn't get a chance to see her too much since Jordan's death. She stands up and motions for her to come over, Reign is equally happy to see her and walks over. Vicky has her arms out ready to give her a big hug, they hug and take a seat.

Vicky with a smile on her face asks, "So how have you been?"

Reign answers, "I'm good, still working at Hoops and Hops, practicing getting ready for summer ball."

Vicky in a more serious tone, "I miss seeing you around, you know sometimes I find myself daydreaming about what might have been."

Reign shakes her head in agreement, "I miss him a lot. Everything that we went through just for him to be killed on the day he comes home seems so unfair." She shakes her head lost in thought.

Ericka and Zoey sitting on the floor looking at Tik-Tok video's looks up at them sensing the somber mood overtaking the room. Ericka, "So mom can I go?

Vicky brought back to reality with the question answers, "I thought we already talked about it. Now's not a good time, maybe another day."

Reign seeing the disappointment in Ericka's face, "I got them it will be my treat they've been talking about Space Slam for two weeks. I'm off today I don't have any plans and I want to see it too."

Ericka hears this and her face lightens up, "Can I go now?" Vicky seeing her happiness finally gives in, "Okay you can go."

Both Ericka and Zoey stand up and hurriedly walk to the door. Zoey yells, "Come on let's go I don't want to be late."

Reign looks at her phone and replies back, "Calm down, we got 45 minutes before the movie starts."

She stands up and tells Vicky, "If you ever want to talk you can text me."

Vicky stands up, looks her in the face, "Thanks and I mean for everything, she grabs her hand and squeezes, "I'm sure Jordan would want you to go on with your life." They hug one last time and they leave, Vicky sits back on the couch with tears welling up in her eyes.

Jackson, Dez, and Brent the same dude that was with them at the basketball court when KJ drew down on them are in the video game section of the Play Day movie-arcade center. It is pretty much empty. A few teenage employees are walking around goofing off on different games, they walk around to the connect four basketball game. Jackson sees three basketballs left in the bin and walks over grabs one and takes a shot he misses. Dez, right behind him grabs the other ball, and shoots nothing but net.

Brent walking away tells them, "I got to go to the bathroom, don't go nowhere."

Jackson asks, "What was up with your pops?" as he grabs the last basketball juggling it back and forth between his hands.

Dez leaning on the game responses, "He's bugging about the beef between me and KJ, saying we going to kill each other or do time. He wants to have a meeting with his mom so we can settle this."

"How you feel?"

"I don't know I can't let this fool just draw down on me and get away with it. Hell, he drew down on you too what are you going to do about it?" Dez's phone rings he stands up off the machine pulls it out of his pocket looks at it shakes his head, tells Jackson, "It figures it's my pops."

"What's up."

Omar in a gruff voice, asks "Boy where you at?" Jackson overhears and chuckles to himself, just glad that his dad is not like that.

"At Play Day."

"I'll be there in 20 minutes to get you, be outside waiting."

Dez protests, "I just got here."

Omar yells, "I don't care, you better be outside don't make me come in there and get you." He hangs up.

Dez pulls the phone away from his ear looks at it mumbles, "I hate him."

Ericka, Zoey, and Reign walk into the Play Day.

Reign walks two to three steps ahead of Zoey and Ericka, Zoey yells out to Reign, "We're going to be in the arcade" she leans on Ericka pushing her towards the arcade.

Reign looks back at them answers, "Don't be in there too long the movie starts in ten minutes."

They don't answer back as they are already in the arcade.

Brent back from the bathroom, asks "So what y'all fools going to do?"

Dez in a salty mood answers, "Damn I can't stay my pops is on his way to pick me up."

Brent asks "Why didn't you tell him you just got here?"

"I did fool I'm going outside and wait for him I don't wanna hear his bitching if I ain't there."

Zoey and Ericka are in the room where all the prizes are kept, looking at the stuffed animals, Zoey looks up and sees Dez Jackson and Brent at the connect four basketball game. Ericka's back is turned she is looking at a large stuffed black cat. Zoey taps her and asks, "Ain't that the boys KJ and Dre got into a fight with at the game?"

Ericka turns around looks answers, "Yeah I need to ask him something." She walks towards him.

6

AS SHE IS WALKING TOWARDS DEZ

Zoey doesn't know what to think so she chases after her.

Ericka approaches Dez who has his back turned away from her looking at the basketball game. Brent and Jackson see her approaching steps aside thinking that she wants to play the game.

Dez seeing them step aside turns around and sees Ericka and Zoey walking towards him.

She walks up to him and asks, "Why do you hate my brother?"

He chuckles a little to himself both amused and surprised by her brashness, looks at both Brent and Jackson, looks back at her, "Who is your brother?"

Ericka answers, "KJ. Y'all got into a fight at the game a few months ago. He was going to shoot you at the basketball courts Friday."

Dez, answers defiantly, "Little girl get lost. Why don't you ask him why he hates me?"

Ericka in a sad voice answers, "I wasn't trying to make you mad, it's just my older brother was already killed and I don't want KJ killed."

Zoey's phone pings and she pulls it out of her backpack looks at tells Ericka, "Reign just texted she is waiting for us at the ticket booth, we got to go."

Ericka looks back at Dez with a blank stare as Zoey pulls on her, she turns and jogs away with her.

All three of them look at them as they run away, Brent shakes his head slowly and says, "Damn dogg that is some deep shit."

Dez thrown off by the exchange, says quietly, "I need to get outside before my dad comes."

As he walks outside, he sees his father's gray Ford f-150 truck approaching. He pulls up to the curb as Dez gets in the truck, his father still in a surly mood comments, "I'm glad I didn't have to come in there and hunt for you."

Dez still thinking about the conversation with Ericka says, "KJ's sister came up to me and asked me why I hate him?"

"So, what did you tell her?"

"I didn't know what to tell her, I told her to ask her brother."

Omar coming to a stoplight looks over at Dez, tells him, "I'm text his mom to set up a meeting."

Dez shrugs his shoulders replies, "Okay, "Where are we going?"

Omar takes off from the traffic light drives two blocks and makes a right in the Krager parking lot, he pulls up to the front of the store and stops. He looks at Dez tells him, "We're here."

Dez confused, "Okay……What are we here for?"

"I need you to drop off my prescription", he reaches into the dashboard storage bin and gives Dez the paper, "Here's my other list," he grabs another paper from the same storage area and gives it to Dez.

He looks at the list, "I didn't want to do no shopping."

Omar answers, "You ain't shopping boy, it's just a couple of things now get out."

Dez opens the door, Omar lets down the window and yells at him, "Don't forget to drop off my script." He lets up the window and drives away.

He finds a parking spot at the end of the lot. He pulls out his phone and looks up Vicky's contact.

He turns on the voice to text on his phone and starts talking *Are you still down to meet to talk about the beef between our kids?*

At home, Vicky's watching, The Payne House on AAET when her phone pings. She reaches over reads the text, shakes her head up and down approvingly thinks, *Okay I guess he was serious.* She grabs her phone and texts back *Yes most def, this needs to end, what are you thinking?*

Omar still waiting on Dez texts back, *I will be going out of town this weekend it will have to be sometime next week. What's a good day for u?*

Vicky still watching tv texts back, *any day besides Tuesday, we need to do it after the boys get out of school so they can be there.*

Bet, What about Friday afternoon at 4?

She texts back, *Sounds good,* she wonders where should we meet, after a few seconds though she continues the text, *we can meet at my house, I will text you the address Thursday.*

Omar reads the text and texts back, *I will get back with you if anything changes.*

He goes back to his game on his phone, two minutes later, Dez comes up to the truck and with both hands full of bags throws them in the back seat. He gets into the truck "Did you have to park so far away?"

Omar starts the truck ignoring the question replies, "We're meeting up with that boy's mom next week."

He remembers Ericka's comment answers quietly, "Whatever."

Vicky gets up off the couch and goes to KJ's room, the door is shut she knocks twice and goes straight in.

He is lying down on his bed playing on his phone, she stands at the door and announces, "I just got finish texting that boy's father who you've been having a problem with, we are meeting with them next week."

He sits up on the bed and exclaims, "What?? Why?"

"To stop y'all from killing each other that's why. What's your problem?"

KJ still sitting up replies, "That nigga's sus and a bully and I just don't like him."

She walks into the room and sits down at his desk, looks at him, "Would you feel more comfortable if your Uncle was at the meeting."

"Yeah, I don't know…. I guess." KJ replies.

"Well give him a call you got his number."

KJ looks at his mom with a sad expression and asks, "Can you do it for me."

She looks back at him with his sad eyes and realizes even though he wants to come off as hard, he is still her little boy. She smiles, "I know exactly what you did, don't think you played me, give me your phone."

He laughs back and gives her the phone.

He picks up the phone after three rings, *"What's up KJ?"*

"This isn't KJ it's Vicky."

"Okay, then What's up Vicky?"

She takes a deep breath and dives right in, *"Well here's the deal we're meeting with that kid that KJ got into a* fight with. We would feel a lot more comfortable if you could be there."

Antonio's in his car, "So what day we talking?"

"Friday at 4, my house."

"That's not really a good time for me with work but I told him if he ever needed me I would be there for him. I will make it happen. Is he there?"

"Yeah, he's right here beside me." She gives him the phone.

He reluctantly takes it, "What's up Unc?"

I've been meaning to hit you up after the situation with that dude, I just wanted to give it some time to settle down. So how do you feel about meeting with him?"

"I don't want too but mom is making me."

"Don't stress about it, I got you, maybe this will put everything to bed once and for all and we can move on."

KJ quietly answers, "If you say so."

"Look I'm headed to a meeting for a potential new client, I will get with you later."

Later Uncle Antonio. He hangs up.

KJ drops the phone on the bed.

"Everything okay."

KJ shakes his head yes. She stands up, looks down at him "Don't worry everything will work out. Let me get in here and check if Ericka called and get dinner going."

She walks out of the room and shuts the door, she picks up her phone looks under recent missed calls and it shows a missed call from the Angelton Prison. She shakes her head slowly dreading why Keith is calling.

7

OMAR DRIVING asks, "So you hungry? "Dez, "Sure."

"What do you think about Chick a Dee?" he asks as he sees one coming up on the right at the next stoplight.

"Cool that will work."

He turns into Chick a Dee and sees the drive-through is full, "We gonna go get it to go even though it's packed they get you through pretty fast."

Dez just shrugs, and answers, "Cool."

Omar pulls into the line, "I talked to my supervisor about switching shifts so, I will be able to be there to get you to school."

"School is school." he continues, "Can I ask you a serious question?"

Omar drives up he is one car length from the menu. "Wait let's order then you can ask."

After a long ten-minute wait, Dez grows impatient, and blurts out, "They must be ordering the entire menu."

Omar chuckles at the comment and Dez realizes this is the first time, he has heard his dad laugh in a long time. Omar replies, "Chill what's the hurry?"

They drive up to the menu, Dez is somewhat hesitant he is not sure how much he should order, asks nervously, "Can I get anything I want?"

Omar sensing his nervousness answers, "Today was payday, go ahead we don't come here too often, just don't get crazy."

A female voice comes over the intercom, "Welcome to Chick-A- Dee can I take your order?"

He smiles looks over at the menu and yells, "Give me the spicy Chicken sandwich and the waffle potato fries with a large lemon aide." Omar's studying the menu, remarks, "Dr. says I need to start eating healthier with my blood pressure but damn those salads are high."

Dez laughingly says "You want to give me advice about what I should do but you don't want to listen to your Dr. about your health?"

Omar's surprised by his comment, laughs back, and answers, "You right." He turns to the menu yells give me a large Cobb salad and a sweet tea."

Over the speaker, the same voice asks, "Is that everything?" Omar answers, "Yes." "Okay drive around I will give you the price at the window."

He drives around and gets their order and they drive away.

Dez is holding the food as Omar is driving the aroma of the food is so strong that he can't resist, so he reaches in the bag and grabs a fry.

Omar in a firm voice, "Don't eat in my truck." Dez's mouth wide open anticipating the fry drops it back in the bag.

Omar driving them home comes back to the earlier conversation, "So what was the question that you wanted to ask?"

"Why do you want to meet up with these people so bad?"

"Well DJ's doing twenty-plus years in the pen for killing this boys' brother, I did 10 years for attempted armed robbery. I just don't want you to end up in prison too. Hopefully, you can be the one to break the cycle of us all doing time. When I was 15 I used to run with the 169 boys we hustled on the corner, cut school, smoked, drinking all the same shit you do now. One night, we were all smoking and drinking some 40's, in T-Bones ride. It was me T-Bone, Shades, and Bam all in the car. Shades comes up with the idea that we need to jack, Steve's Beer and Wine. I was the youngster in the car, everybody else was around eighteen, nineteen. T-Bone gave me his piece, bam had his. Me and Bam got out while T-Bone and Shades waited in the car. We walked in and Bam pulls his piece out and points it at Steve. He pushes me to empty the register while he watched the door. Mr. Steve was in the store by himself, he must not be feeling well because he was coughing a lot when we came in. I run behind the register and have Mr. Steve open it, I was emptying the register when out of nowhere, his partner comes in through the door that Bam was supposed to be watching. He has a sawed off and blasts the door barely missing him.

Dez caught up in the story, "What happened?"

Omar turns into the Hill Point Apartments, "Well T-Bone and Shades see this and take off leaving me and Bam. Bam at the door pushes the dude out the way and he falls Bam then takes off. I tried to make a break for the door, but before I get to the door, both Steve and his partner had me covered with guns I was stuck until the police came and arrested me."

They pull up to the front of the apartment, Omar tells him, "You grab the bags I will get the drinks." They both get out of the truck and go to the house, after they sit down at the table, Dez asks, "Did you snitch on them?"

Omar offended by the question, "I know the streets! You don't snitch! I'm the one that got caught, so I did the time. Shaking his head as he is talking "Now that I look back at it I don't have a damn thing to show for it. All the time I was locked up not one of them called... visited... nothing... I was just another nigga locked up."

"So, what they up to now?"

"I don't know or care, when I got out I heard that Shades is doing time for robbing a bank I guess he didn't learn nothing from my deal. T-Bone is on the run and I don't know what's up with Bam."

Dez takes a sip of his drink says, "Crazy story, but what's that got to do with me?"

Omar shakes his head in frustration blurts out, "So you don't see any kind of connection? I don't know if you are stupid or blind. I've done time, your brothers doing time. You got some boy about to shoot you, you been arrested for fighting in school, you skipping school, everything you're doing I was doing at your age, the only difference is I had no one around to tell me the right thing to do. You got lucky he didn't shoot you but what about the next time? It ain't even got to be this boy it could be somebody else, at some point, you got to be sick of living that life. I know I did, All I got to show for it is 10 years I will never get back, high blood pressure a wife who up and ran out on me. Last but not least two sons, who are trying to get buried before I do."

He gets up from the table and walks away lighting up a cigarette. Before he leaves the kitchen, he turns around announces, "Don't make any plans Saturday were going to visit your brother."

8

VICKY'S PHONE PINGS SHE HAS just gotten a text. Her laptop's open ready to log on. KJ and Ericka are at school and she's about to go online to research interviewing skills. It has been about 10 years since she has had a job interview.

She gets her phone off the coffee table. She looks at the text, *This is Helen with, Dr. Murvin's office, we had a cancellation, one p.m. is now open if you would still like an appointment call me as soon as you can.*

Vicky immediately calls after the second ring the phone is answered, *"Good morning this is Helen with Dr. Murvin's office. How can I assist you?"*

Vicky excitedly responds, *"Um yes I'm Vicky Skyy returning the text about making an appointment. I would like to come in today if it is still possible."*

"Sure, so you can make it today at one?"

"Yes, it will be no problem I'm just at home about to do some work on the computer."

"Dr. Murvin's 1 pm had to cancel unexpectedly so she wanted to check to see if you could come in."

"As long as we're finished before school gets out so I can be home for my kids."

"*That should be no problem Dr. Murvin has another appointment at two so you should be good.*"

Vicky takes a deep breath and tells her, "*I got fired recently so I don't have insurance.*"

"*Yeah Dr. Murvin's aware, this appointment will be pro bono.*"

Vicky touched by this act of kindness, answers, "*Thank you so much as soon as I get back on my feet I will pay you.*"

Helen answers, "*We good we'll see you at one. Bye.*"

"*Bye.*"

She shuts her laptop, thinks, *I might as well take a shower and freshen up.*

As Vicky approaches the building, the same nervous anxiety she had the first time she visited starts to creep through her body. She gets into the elevator the door opens she pushes the button eighth-floor button. She's alone in the elevator. After getting off the elevator she passes by the bathroom and feels the same urge as before. She goes in to compose herself, takes a few deep breaths looks in the mirror, mumbles quietly, "Why am I nervous, I'm a queen I got this." She leaves and walks down the hall and goes into the office. It is the same setup as before.

She walks to the receptionist desk who is texting on her phone she looks up at Vicky and asks," Are you, Mrs. Skyy?"

Vicky answers, "Yes I'm here for my appointment with Dr. Murvin."

The receptionist answers back, "I'm Helen nice to meet you. You can take a seat I will let Brenda know you are here." She immediately picks up the phone.

Vicky walks away towards the waiting room chairs, before she even gets to them Dr. Murvin struts down the hallway to meet her, with a smile on her face and motioning with her right hand, "Come on back."

Vicky makes a beeline and follows behind Brenda into her office, She shuts the door, she then immediately turns around and before Vicky can go Dr. Murvin grabs her and gives her a tremendous hug. This startles her yet she relishes it, has been a minute since she has had a hug like this.

After a minute she lets go, Vicky smiling, "Is that how you say hello

to all your patients?"

"I'm sorry it just when I heard about what happened I felt you needed that."

Vicky walks over to the couch and takes a seat, "I did."

Dr. Murvin takes a seat on the matching chase, "It's been a month since we last talked and I know a little about what happened. Would you like to talk more about it?"

She lets out a sigh and answers, "That's what I'm here for" she continues, "I remember it was Jordan's birthday and I just woke up with an odd vibe, Me and the kids decided to observe his heavenly birthday by visiting his gravesite. KJ wasn't comfortable with it so his Uncle Antonio was going to join us. I go to work so far pretty much a normal day, after lunch while working in the emergency room, I have to deal with this racist, 'Karen' who kept calling me a nigger. I tried to keep my cool but she kept pushing my buttons. I snapped and was about to teach her some manners. A coworker restrained me, next thing I know I was in HR getting fired!"

"Then what happened?"

"Well, I go home, and once there I was in a state of shock realizing that I had just got fired and not knowing what I was going to do. I'm in my room my mind is racing I then get a call from Antonio, telling me that he can't find KJ and this sends me over the edge, thinking the worst like he had been killed. I don't know how to describe what happened it was like I was in a trance, between getting fired especially on Jordan's birthday then KJ's missing I felt like I couldn't deal with it anymore so I walked into my bathroom and grabbed some sleeping pills and. ..."

Dr. Murvin sits there quietly scribbling on her notepad gives Vicky a chance to regain her composure.

"So how close were you to going through with it?"

I don't know, I had the bottle in my hand as I said earlier I was in a 'trance' hearing Ericka's happy voice snapped me out of it. My brother Antonio shows up and we go looking for KJ. We found him with a gun about to shoot the brother of the boy who killed Jordan."

Dr. Murvin leans forward excitedly "So what happened?"

"Well, I and his Uncle talked him into giving us the gun before he shot him."

Dr. Murvin sits back in the chair and breathes a sigh of relief "Thank

God, I can't imagine what that would have done to you."

Vicky sits there not even wanting to think about how it would have affected her.

Dr. Murvin moves on to not give her too much time to dwell on the question asks "So how have you been doing since that day?"

Vicky looks at her and smiles then replies, "Good a lot better, both my brother and his wife have been there for support. I talked with my kids a little about it. Even though I'm not working right now I feel good I got an interview set up for next week and I'm going to get this job and get back on my feet."

Dr. Murvin's pleasantly surprised by Vicky's shot of confidence tells her, "That's it believe it and it will happen. Speak it into existence," as she shakes her head with approval. "You said you told the kids about it so how much did you tell them?"

"I talked about it real briefly I wasn't sure how much I should tell them. You think I should talk to them more about it?"

"I think it is good that you spoke with them about it so they can be aware, as far as how much you should tell them that is something you will have to decide, I do remember you saying that your daughter Ericka was mature for her age."

"Well to be honest with you she is not the one I'm worried about."

"Yeah well based on what you told me I can see why" they both laugh. Dr. Murvin continues, "It appears like you have general anxiety disorder. The inability to move on with your life over Jordan's death, the constant fear of the same thing happening to KJ, and then losing your job did not help the situation. So how long has Jordan been gone?"

"Nine months, why you ask?"

Dr. Murvin takes a moment before she answers wanting to find the right words, looks directly at her, "It's been nine months, so what's holding you back from moving on with your life?"

Vicky annoyed by this, answers, "I am living my life, what do you mean?"

Dr. Murvin sees her change in demeanor replies, "Look I'm not going to pretend to know what you are going through but I know it is not healthy to obsess. You have to go on with your life for yourself and your kids. You have plenty of years left to live, I know you want to be there when they graduate, get married, have kids, and make you a grandmother."

Vicky shakes her head in agreement, "Yeah I definitely do."

"Closure." Dr. Murvin blurts out.

"What?"

"That's what you and KJ need is… closure." Dr. Murvin replies.

What's is closure?"

"I really can't answer that, closure will probably mean something different for each of you."

She thinks about what she said and finally answers, "Maybe your right."

"Are you taking any medications?"

"No, I have been taking some ST. Johns Wort I got at the store."

"I think we need to try something different."

Dr. Murvin gets up out of the chase and walks behind her desk opens a drawer gets a key and opens a locked med closet. She pulls out a small white box and places it on the desk.

"So, what's this?"

"Effexor XR for your anxiety."

Dr. Murvin walks over and gives it to Vicky tells her, "This is a 30- day trial subscription, the directions are on the back."

Vicky takes the package and puts it beside her cell phone. She stands up, "Are there any side effects?"

"Well like any prescription medication, you take there is the chance of some side effects, skin rashes, or hives. Blurred vision, coughing tightness in your chest, dizziness, trouble sleeping, and a few other things. There are some other symptoms that you have to be on the lookout for, just read the package."

Vicky jokes "Well I'm experiencing some of these without the medicine."

Beep! Beep! Dr. Murvin's phone alarm goes off, Vicky hearing this laughs, "I know what that means."

Dr. Murvin chuckles, "I'm sorry, but I had to squeeze you."

"No worries, I am just so thankful for you being able to see me today. You have given me a lot to think about."

Dr. Murvin steps closer and hugs Vicky, "I know this is not professional but we started the session with this, so we can end it like this."

Vicky smiles and returns the hug after ten seconds. Dr. Murvin releases her, "Well I got my next appointment in ten minutes."

Vicky grabs her cell phone and the medication. "I understand."

Dr. Murvin walks to the medication closet locks it, "Call me if you have any problems."

"Ok," she walks out of the office and down the hallway. In the waiting room, there is a black couple that looks to be in their mid-30's waiting. Helen to Vicky as she walks out, "Will you need another appointment?"

Vicky stops by the desk, "I'm sure I will I will have to give you a call I have a job interview coming up and I don't know what days I will be available."

Helen looks up at her, "Good luck, and just let us know."

Vicky walks out and, flips open her cell phone holder, and sees she has a missed call from her sister Michelle, she goes to her voicemail and sees she has left a message, "*I just got off the phone with Antonio, he told me everything going on. Just wanted to check in to let you know I'm with you, call me when you get this message."* She hangs up and flips her phone holder close thinks, *I will call her from the car.*

Driving on her way home, she calls Michelle after five rings the call goes to voicemail, she leaves a message, "*Sorry I missed your call I was at a Dr.'s appointment, everything's good girl, I'm just trying to get another job if you got any leads to let me know. Alright, talk to you later."*

As she is driving home she turns on the radio to the Steve Harvey show, her phone rings, she hits the pickup button on the steering wheel.

"Hello?"

"What's up baby it's Keith."

9

VICKY SHOCKED THAT KEITH'S ON THE phone stutters, "What's up?"

Keith catching her nerves, "What's wrong? Why you all anxious?"

She answers, *"I'm not anxious I just was expecting a call from Michelle."*

"So how is Michelle? I haven't heard from her in years."

Vicky interrupts him, *"Cut the bullshit, Keith. What do want?"*

"Yeah cool, I don't get a lot of time anyway, you know the last time we talked I told you I might be getting out in two months well I got some time dropped because of good behavior."

Vicky sarcastically answers, *"Well good for you. You do remember that I hung up on you the last time we talked."*

"Aw come on girl, don't be like that, I thought you'd be happy. I'm hoping we can give it another shot."

Vicky hears this and she feels her anxiety rising, her hands start to tremble, she pulls up to the stoplight hits the right blinker, she needs to pull over.

Her voice raises, *"What about that hoe you went down to Houston with? I got too much shit going on right now, I just got fired, KJ's out in here in the streets a wannabe gangster. Now you drop this on me about wanting to get back together? You always have had perfect timing."* The light turns green and she turns into a Wal store parking lot.

"You talking about Madison?? She was just some jump-off I was hanging with for the weekend she meant nothing. Relax chill baby you don't have to decide today. I just wanted to reach out and give you a heads up."

Vicky sitting in her car regaining her composure in a calmer voice answers, *"I don't know I got too much wrong going on in my life to add another thing to it."*

"Like I said no pressure just think about it. Well, my time is about up. I will call you next week please pick up, if I didn't know better I think you were avoiding my call."

She laughs to herself at the comment, *"Okay I need to go to get on this computer, Bye."*

She's home and sits in the driveway and takes a moment to think about the conversation and if she should tell the kids. She gets out of the car shaking her head as she thinks about KJ's possible reaction to the news.

It's a breezy Saturday morning Omar's driving his truck down a long two-lane road and Dez is asleep in the passenger seat. Omar with his right hand shakes Dez's left shoulder to wake him up.

Dez groggily wakes up yells, "What? What?" as he straightens himself up in the seat.

Omar focused on the road tells him, "We are almost there about 15 minutes away."

Dez stretches out and yawns ask, "What time is it? How long have we been riding?"

"About four hours and it's 930. Our visitation is scheduled for 1030."

"So why are we getting there so early?"

"Look we need to be early these people are very strict, we traveled over 300 miles to see him and I can't take a chance because we got there 5 minutes late."

Dez asks in disbelief, "They really wouldn't let us see him because we are five minutes late?"

Omar answers, "Hell yeah, I've seen them turn people down because their driver's license is expired. Women wearing the wrong clothing or too much jewelry these people don't play."

"What do we have to do once we get there?"

Omar passes a sign on the road that reads *Wallace/Ware Prison Unit 10 miles.*

Dez sees the sign and he's getting a nervous tingling inside.

Omar, "Well after we park make sure you have your id. You did bring your school id like I told you right?"

He pulls a blue and gold lanyard out of his front right pocket and on the end of it is his school id, he dangles it out for Omar to see replies, "Yes it's right here."

"Good I hate to have to leave you in the car while I'm in visitation. Well, we empty our pockets of everything except the money, car keys, and ID. Lock the doors,"

Dez asks, "Money?"

"Yeah, I'm putting fifty dollars on his card."

"Card?? What Card??"

Omar is getting a little frustrated with the 20 questions but he realizes that this is Dez's first time and he is curious. He answers, "It's like a debit card for prisoners. You put money on it so they can buy stuff. Once we get to the building we have to sign in with our names. The inmate we going to visit, their D.O.C. number. Our car info and then we sit and wait till they call us. When they call us up we have to show them our ID's and they check them against their visitation log. We then have to empty our pockets into a bucket and walk through a metal detector."

As they continue driving on the left-hand side of the road there is a big open field about 600 yards from the road and a twenty-foot-high fence with concertina wire at the very top. Within the fence are about six or seven blue aluminum buildings some of the buildings are single-story while others are two to three stories tall they all have white aluminum roofs. On the corner outside the fence is a gray concrete guard tower four stories tall with the same metal roof as the other buildings. Two prison guards are standing outside keeping watch.

Dez sees this and is getting nervous. Omar looks over at him and says, "Well we're almost here." He drives down the road for about another thirty seconds, the road is pretty much empty so he makes the left turn into a long road with a sign that reads **Dick Ware Unit Texas Department of Criminal Justice.**

10

AS OMAR BACKS HIS TRUCK INTO the parking spot Dez notices a prison SUV creeping along in the lot driving along slowly checking out each vehicle's tag.

He sees Dez watching the vehicle tells him, "They're just checking each plate to make sure they are registered in their system." He finishes parking, and opens up the center console, "Place everything in your pockets in here except your id."

Dez pulls out his cell phone and drops it in the console, Omar grabs his wallet pulls out his driver's license and a single $50, then places his wallet and cell in the console.

Both are walking towards the main gate between the parked cars neither one talking both lost in their thoughts, Dez is about 10 yards ahead of Omar. He yells out, to Dez "Slow down, you know I can't move as fast as I used to."

He doesn't say anything he stops on the sidewalk next to the gate and lets out a sigh.

Omar catches up with him out of breath tells him, "That's what's wrong with you kids today always in a rush even when you don't know where you're going."

Before they get to the gate there is a small black speaker box and a woman is already there waiting, she looks back at them and gives a polite smile without saying a word.

There is a buzz and a click at the gate a voice over the speaker, instructs, "Ms. Johnson you can come in." She walks up pulls on the handle opens it up and walks through. Dez is about to follow her through when, the intercom booms, "Stop! Shut the gate! Do not do anything until you are instructed to." Dez startled by this shuts the gate. Omar admonishes him, "This is a prison boy, I told you they don't play."

After a five-minute wait, the voice comes back on the intercom asks, "Are you two together? What are your names?"

Omar answers, "I'm Omar Russell and this is my son Dezera and we're here to see my other son Dejuan Russell."

"Stand by," the voice says over the intercom.

Omar looks at Dez tells him, "This is why we needed to be early."

"Okay Omar and Dezera come in," the voice says as the gate is buzzed and clicked.

They both walk through the gate and Omar makes sure to shut it as an older couple is approaching it.

They walk into the building through automatic sliding glass doors. Inside the room is a row of seven multicolor plastic chairs connected by a metal bar at the bottom. There are four rows of chairs on each side of the room. They are facing a stand-up counter with two computers on them and two COs are standing up typing on them. Just to the left behind them is a walk-through metal detector the kind like they have in airports, behind the detectors in an electronic door with a small 12x12 window in the center.

About 10 people are sitting in the chairs. Omar and Dez walk to the counter. There is an older male CO at the counter he looks to be in his late forty's, early fifties. When they walk up, "Who you here to see?"

Omar answers, "Dejuan Russell."

The COs begin typing and instruct them, "I need to see both of your IDs."

They both pull out their IDs and place them on the counter, the officer picks up Omar's license and typing on the computer says, "We already have a copy of your license on file." He gives it back to Omar he then picks up Dez's school ID looks at it and asks, "How old are you?"

"Fourteen."

He looks at him like he doesn't believe him. He puts Dez's ID on a scanner connected to the computer and gives it back to him.

The CO then hands Omar a sheet of paper and pen and tells him, "Fill in the info about your car sign it and give it back to me."

He then passes another sheet to Dez, "Here read this and sign it at the bottom."

"What's this?"

"Visitation Rules all first-time visitors have to sign it."

He grabs the paper, looks at them without reading as soon as Omar finishes with the pen he grabs it and signs the paper, and passes it back to the guard.

The guard knows he didn't read it but doesn't care, he looks at Omar and tells him, "I see that your visitation is set up for 1030 you still have ten minutes. If you got any money to put on his J-Card you can use the kiosk to the left to load it up." He points to two kiosks on the left in the back, "You need to load up his card before the visitation."

Omar, "Ok thank you" and walks towards the kiosk, Dez walks to the chairs.

He finishes at the kiosk and takes the seat next to Dez, "Well now it's just a hurry up and wait time."

Dez slouches down in the chair, "Okay whatever. So how long do we have for visitation?"

"Four hours since we had to come from over 3 hours away"

Dez lets out a sigh inquires, "Are we going to be here all day?"

Omar, "Boy you haven't seen him in almost a year one day ain't gonna kill you."

He looks up at the clock above the correction officers at sees it 1030. The same officer who processed them calls out, "Russell!"

Omar stands up, and signals for Dez to get up, "Why are you still sitting? Let's go see your brother."

He gets up and they walk to the counter, the officer typing on the keyboard doesn't look up and points towards the metal detectors.

There are two CO officers at the detectors one a female and the other a male.

The male steps up to the table where there are several small plastic baskets on it. He tells them, "Empty your pockets into the basket and take off your shoes." They both empty their pockets putting their ID's and Omar drops in the car keys. They both take off their shoes, the male officer takes the basket and puts it on the other side of the detector he picks up Omar's shoes and passes them to the female officer on the other side of the detector. She has on a pair of plastic gloves, she takes each shoe looks through them shakes them, and places them on the table. They both walk through the detector without any problems.

As they are putting their stuff back on the male officer announces, "Alright y'all good to go."

Omar looks at Dez asks, "You ready?"

11

THE FEMALE OFFICER PUSHES A BUTTON FOR the intercom talking into the speaker, "Two for Russell coming in." She pushes the button the door clicks, as it opens she tells them, "Go through."

Both Dez and Omar step into an empty room painted white about the size of a small bathroom on the other wall is another door a male officer is on the other side and opens it up.

They step through the door and the visitation area, it has a gray carpet with three rows of small white 3x3 metal tables connected at the base to four metal stools at each table. There are six tables in each row. The walls are painted off white to match the tables, there are two vending machines beside each other on the east wall and another two machines on the left side of the door that they came through.

There is a white counter in the rear of the where there are two CO's standing behind it. In each corner of the room is a CO keeping watch.

The CO points at the counter, tells them, "You need to go check-in."

As they walk to the counter inside there are about ten prisoners in their prison Orange jumpsuits having a visitation. Most of them are sitting with women and children. One of them is an elderly couple probably in their seventies he is holding his wife's hand. Dez looks at them and thinks, *That dude could die any day they should let him go.*

They both walk to the counter, Omar tells the officer, "We're here for Dejuan Russell. Here's his J card." He hands it to the CO.

The officer, "Okay, we're getting him now you can grab a seat at a table."

Omar sees an empty table right in front of the visitation counter and takes a seat at the table. Dez is not happy with the choice as he sits down.

They both sit there quietly, Dez asks, "How long does it take for DJ to get here?"

"I don't know five, ten minutes it all depends."

Another three minutes pass when a door opens up, Omar and Dez turn around, and see DJ with his orange prison suit being escorted by a CO.

They both stand up, Dez's so excited to see DJ yells, "What's up DJ?" and he runs up and hugs him. DJ's equally excited leans down and hugs him back, yells "What's up baby bro?"

Omar stands there smiling feeling good seeing his two sons together even if is during a prison visitation.

After about ten seconds they let go and Dez looks at DJ and sees his left eye is slightly swollen and purple and he has a cut on his lip. He asks, "What happened?"

"I'll tell you at the table, I need to go say hi to pops."

He walks over to the table where Omar is still waiting and smiling without saying a word he places his hands-on on DJ's shoulders with his arm extended looks at DJ slowly shakes his head back and forth and hugs him.

They all sit down at the table. Omar looks at DJ shakes his head, "You got into a scrap huh?"

"Yeah."

Omar still shaking his head answers, "I don't miss those days."

Dez excitedly inquires, "What happened?"

"A week ago, in the chow hall, a new boot wanted to test me I guess because I'm one of the youngest here. He stepped up to me at dinner and tried to eat my chocolate cake, he said nothing just stuck his hand in my tray trying to grab my cake. I grabbed his hand and pushed it away. He just picked up his tray and smashed me in the face with it. I was caught off guard and put my head down trying to protect myself. He hit me in the back of the head before my celly tackled him and the CO's snatched him up."

Omar depressed to hear this replies, "Times change but lock up don't. Same shit different pile."

Dez, "So did you get him back?"

"I haven't had a chance he's been in solitary, I haven't seen him."

"What are you going to do when you see him?"

"I don't know I don't want to say too much with all these CO's in here."

Omar looks at DJ, "Remember revenge is a dish best served cold."

Dejuan looks at him and shakes his head in agreement. Dez looks around confused, Omar tells him, "Don't worry about it."

Dez mumbles under his breath and shakes his head.

Dejuan to Omar, "So what's been up at home?"

Omar looks at DJ tells him, "Same old stuff work, school, he takes a deep breath there is something I want to tell you, "I finally was able to contact your mother through Facebook."

Dejuan's excited to hear this ask, "What did she say?"

"She asked me why I was telling her this, when I told I thought she would like to know what is going on with her son. He takes a deep breath and continues, she says, "He's not my son anymore, and hangs up on me."

Dejuan hearing this looks down at the table, fighting back tears. He lifts his head takes a deep sallow, "I'm going get something from the vending machine."

He goes to the counter and gets his J-Card from the CO's then goes to the vending machine gets a bag of Funyon's,

Doritos, a Hersey candy bar, and a Pipeline Punch Monster.

He comes back to the table completely composed sits down mumbles, "Cool, Cool." Looks at Dez asks, "So what's up with you?"

Omar answers abruptly, "I'll tell you what's up with him! That boy's brother who you killed pulled a gun on him a few weeks ago."

Dez jumps in says, "I'm take care of it."

Dejuan slams his fist on the table, startling everybody during the visitation causing them to look over at their table, The CO from behind the counter comes around and asks, "Is everything okay here?"

Omar looks up at the CO answers, "Everything is fine my son just got a little excited. We good."

He does a once-over of the table and goes back behind the counter.

Dejuan stares intently at Dez, "Do you want to end up in here?"

Dez replies, "Just a minute ago you were talking about getting back at the fool who did that to your face. Now you tell me I gotta be a punk?"

"Listen, in here it's a different world, I got at least thirty years if I get punked now I will be fighting to get my rep back for the rest of my time. I need to do this to show I'm not going to be anybody's bitch. You got a chance to avoid all this if you can do the right thing. You don't want this life, I don't want this life but it's too late for me but not you."

Omar interjects, "That's what I been telling him."

Dejuan continues, "Bro prison ain't the place you want to be." He points at his bruised eye, "This ain't shit with some of the stuff I've seen. About two weeks after I got here a ChoMo jumped off the third-floor headfirst and killed himself."

Dez asks "What's a 'ChoMo'?"

Omar answers "Child molester."

DJ continues, "When new meth addicts come in, some of the old heads lick their sores because of the shit that oozes out of them. They still trying to get that high."

Dez hearing this shakes his head in disbelief, "Really??"

DJ opens up the Monster and takes a gulp.

"Dudes be giving hand jobs in the shower so they won't get raped. Hopefully, you are cool with your celly or you can be fighting every day, and I haven't even talked about the gangs and dirty CO.'s. That's all I got to look forward to for the next thirty years. You don't have to if you just listen."

Omar sees this is messing with Dez's head puts his hand up to signal him to stop.

Dejuan opens up the bag of Doritos starts eating and takes another swig of his Monster.

Omar tells Dejuan, "Chill son take it easy, I've set up a meeting with his mom so we can talk this out before something bad happens."

Dejuan opens up, "You know the night it all happened. I remember going over to Reign's house to talk with her after she got off work and he just showed up. I didn't even know he was going to be there. We were talking and he pushed me on the ground and took off running, it was like an unconscious reaction. I blacked out I was just so salty. I saw him lying on the ground, I didn't know what to do, so I took off. I knew I had to get rid of the gun, I didn't want to throw it away cause the police might find it. I dropped it off at Tristan's to hold. I go home and a few hours later the police show up and take me in for questions. Now you tell me Dez might get killed because of me." He pauses for a few seconds to compose himself looks at Omar, "You said you got a meeting with them?"

"Yeah, we haven't got a set time, hopefully sometime next week."

Dejuan sits there staring into space lost in his thought asks the question that surprises Omar, "Do you think that they would come to visit me?"

12

VICKY'S SITTING ON HER BED, laptop open browsing through articles on doing interviews she is nervous about tomorrow.

She looks at the clock at the bottom of the screen it's 830 pm. She takes a deep breath, thinks, *"I've been at this for almost two hours what I don't know by now I will never know."*

She closes her computer gets up and goes to the closet to pick out her outfit for tomorrow. Based on her research she is going with the safe conservative black slacks and a white blouse with a pair of black flats. As she is going through her closet, she picks out a long-sleeved collared shirt, *thinks this should work,* and drops it on the bed.

As she continues to go through her closet, her phone beeps. She goes around the bed grabs it from the nightstand and looks at it. It's from the Angelton State Corrections Center. As it's beeping in her hand she's debating if she should answer it.

She takes a deep breath and pushes the green phone button.

After the standard recording that comes with prison calls. She asks in an irritated tone, *"Why you calling so late?"*

Keith answers, *"I was just checking to see if you gave any more thought about what we talked about."*

"No. Like I told you I got a lot going on. I'm looking for a job, trying to raise two kids by myself one of them your son that you left."

"How many times do I have to apologize for it? I was young and stupid not ready to settle down. I wasn't there for Jordan give me a chance to be there for KJ."

She sits down on the bed and hears the pain and desperation in his voice.

Before she gets a chance to say anything he continues, *"I told you I got some cash hidden away and I can help you get back straight."*

She quietly answers, *"Just give me some time to process things. I got a lot going on and I need to tell the kids to get their thoughts."*

"Of course, I understand, it's just I need to let the staff here know I have somewhere to go by next week."

"I will talk with the kids soon and will take it from there."

"Okay, it's almost lights out so I got to go take care and have a goodnight boo."

Vicky hearing him talk sexy reminds her of some of the good times, but she is cool. *"Goodnight Keith."*

She lays down on the bed giving deep thought about the conversation with Keith, *It would be nice to have someone to help with the bills, and KJ does deserve the chance to have a dad. I just don't know if I can trust him.*

The next morning, she walks to breakfast in her robe where Ericka and KJ are already at the table eating toaster waffles.

Ericka looks at her and asks, "You not taking us to school today?"

Vicky taking a seat answers a little excited, "No I got to get ready I have a job interview today."

Ericka excited, "Cool, good luck." KJ less excited answers, "Yeah, good luck."

Vicky used to KJ's drab mood doesn't react.

Ericka "So where is it at?"

"St. Andrews. Do you think you can get a ride with Zoey?"

Ericka, "Yeah I better text her now." She gets up and goes to get her phone.

Looking at KJ asks, "You ok with riding the bus?"

"It's cool."

Ericka comes back to the kitchen texting on her phone, looks up at Vicky "They are about to leave in 15 minutes so I need to be going."

"Before you go there is something I need to tell the both of you. I was talking" …. she stops in mid-sentence thinks, *Maybe this isn't the best time especially telling KJ I don't need him to do anything crazy at school.*

She gets up and pulls on KJ to get up, "Get up and walk your sister down to Zoey's house, she can't be late. KJ caught off guard shoves the last piece of waffle in his mouth, answers, "Chill what's wrong with you?"

She's still a little flustered from what she was about to tell them, "Nothing just a little nervous about the interview that's all."

Ericka curious, "So what were you going to tell us?"

Vicky replies, "Nothing." as she shakes her head, "It can wait until after you get home. Now go get your backpacks and go. Love you both." She gets up and starts clearing the table.

They walk to their rooms get their backpacks and leave.

Walking down the street to Zoey's house, Ericka asks, "What do you think mom was going to tell us?"

KJ nonchalantly "I don't know and don't care."

They approach the front yard, Zoey and Reign are walking to the car. Ericka runs across the yard to the front of the car.

KJ continues walking, Reign sees KJ and yells out to him, "Do you want a ride?"

He stops and looks back at them, "Nah I'm good."

About three hundred yards away he sees the bus is already at the stop loading up. Dre is the last person getting on the bus, he sees KJ walking towards the bus. After he gets on the bus, the door shuts. KJ sees this and takes off running to the bus. The bus does not take off. He makes it to the door and the driver opens it up.

The bus driver yells, "You almost got left and that's a long walk, your boy Dre told me you were coming."

Dre sitting right behind the driver says, "We good fam."

KJ sits, directly across from him, "So you ain't salty?"

"Bro I wasn't the one that was salty."

"Yeah I know, sometimes I bug out."

Dre inquires, "You and Dez good now?"

"I guess. I ain't seen him in about two weeks. We ran into each other at the PO's office he was talking shit. His dad and my mom talked they want us to all get-together and bury it."

"Sounds like a good idea. You don't want to do that?"

"I don't know. I just don't like that fool."

"He might be cool you and him could be bros after you get to know him."

KJ sarcastically replies, "Yeah sure. Can you let Storm know we good so she won't block me?"

"Yeah, I got you." They dap each other up.

Vicky wearing her black slacks and long sleeve white blouse and black flats sits on the second floor of the St. Andrews Medical Center Human Resource Office. It is a sterilized office with a light blue carpet and three gray cloth chairs in front of a white counter with three associates behind the counter typing away on computers. Inside the office are four more offices with their doors closed. She pulls her phone out of her black tote, she flips open her phone case, it's nine forty-five.

She sees that Shea has sent her a text, *Good luck at the interview, get with me afterward to let me know how it went.*

She puts her phone back in her tote.

She puts the tote back on the floor beside her chair. The wait is killing her. She starts reading over her resume.

The office door directly to her left opens up and a gentleman who looks to be in his forties in a blue suit and red tie. Walks to her and ask, "Mrs. Skyy?"

Vicky answers, "Yes."

"If you're ready we can get the interview going."

She gets up takes a deep breath and picks up her tote. He tells her, "You can leave your purse with the receptionist if you like."

She answers, "Okay," and places it on the counter.

She follows him into a conference room, it has a twenty-foot long table with three high back black leather rolling chairs on each side and one chair at each end of the table. Inside are two women one wearing a matching gray skirt and jacket outfit the other wearing a peach-colored pants suit. Both sit on the other side of the table, quietly observing everything.

The gentleman who escorted her in tells her, "Shut the door please." She closes the door.

13

"WELL IF THERE ARE NOT ANY MORE

questions I think that concludes this interview,' the woman in the peach outfit replies.

Vicky sits there trying to think of something else, shakes her head no, answers, "Not that I can think of."

"Well, I guess that's it."

All three of them get up and come around the table to shake her hand.

She stands up as they approach her and shakes each of their hands, "When can I expect to hear something back?"

The man answers, "If you are selected to move on we will be in touch by sometime late next week."

He then opens the conference room door for her, she turns and tells them, "I want to thank you for the chance to interview for this position."

They all smile at her as she walks out of the room.

She gets her purse and leaves.

As she walks out of the office she looks in her tote for her phone to check for messages.

There is a text from, Shea, *Checking in with you to see how the interview went.*

She gets to her car, texts back *Just finished the interview I feel good.*

She gets in her car and starts to drive home. As she approaches a stoplight she gets another text from Shea: *What you up to now?*

Vicky using the voice to text feature on her phone answers, *I'm on the way home to get out of these clothes.*

Her phone rings she knows who it is she pushes the phone button on her steering wheel. Shea blurts out, *"Why don't you come by Antonios? Where here just chillin."*

"I don't know I just want to get out of these shoes."

"You can take your shoes off here, it's just me and Ant in the office he's doing some work on the computer I'm here bored come on through we haven't talked in a week."

Vicky looks at her car clock it's 1255 she thinks, *I don't have any plans I just need to be home before they get home from school.*

"I'll be there in 15 minutes."

"Alright girl see you then." Shea hangs up.

Vicky pulls into **Antonio's Fit Club** there are five cars in the lot she parks on the left side of Shea's white BMWx5.

As she walks into Antonio's fitness center, she realizes she does not recognize it. He has renovated since the last time she was here. Once you enter the building there is a red counter and behind it are two gentlemen talking to each other one white and one black they are both wearing red t-shirts with Antonio's Fit Club written in white block lettering. The black associate sees Vicky walk in and immediately steps up and tells her, "Welcome to Antonio and Shea's Fit Club. How can I assist you?"

Vicky walks up to the counter, "I'm here to see my brother Antonio and Shea."

"They are in the office, I can show you the way."

He walks from behind the counter, Vicky notices his name is Rodney from his id badge. He is about 6'1" dark-skinned muscled up. His hair is cut short with a taper fade, there is some gray that is starting to creep in on the sides, he has a full chin strap beard that's peppered with gray. He's wearing a small diamond earring in his left ear. She waits till his back is turned and checks him out. He has on a pair of black workout shorts, a small smile forms on her face. As they are walking through the middle of the fitness center, he turns around, looks at her, "What's up I'm Rodney Mellers."

She answers back sarcastically, "Yeah, I saw your name tag."

"Your Antonio's younger sister?"

"Don't you know it's impolite to ask a woman's age?"

"I wasn't asking your age I was just making an observation." They arrive at the office in the back of the building. He knocks on a door and opens it up. It's a small office with two desks right beside each other. Antonio is sitting at the one on the far left typing on a computer, Shea is at the other desk talking with Antonio.

Rodney to Antonio, "Your sister Vicky is here to see you."

Antonio does not look up he continues typing, "I got some potential new clients that are coming by in 30 minutes. I need you to show them around."

"Got it," he looks at Vicky smiling says to her, "It was nice meeting you Vicky hope to see you again."

She smiles back at him, "Nice meeting you Rodney." He leaves and shuts the door. Vicky goes to sit on a black couch on the left side of the desk Shea is at.

Shea watching the flirting going on laughs, "Girl he's feelin you."

Vicky laughs back, "You know I don't have time for that."

"You need to make time, ain't that right boo?"

Without looking up from the computer, he answers, "Yeah right boo."

She knows he's not paying attention so she turns back to Vicky, who has taken off her shoes and laid down on the couch, "So how did the interview go?"

"Well I felt good about it but you can never tell. I was interviewed by three people in a big board room. You can never get a feel for the room everybody is so robotic,"

"That's done on purpose to intimidate you."

"Well, it worked."

"Don't get discouraged keep the grind up, you'll get something. What else has been up?"

Vicky sits up on the couch, "Have I told you that Keith has been calling trying to get back together?"

Antonio hears this and stops typing looks up at Vicky, Shea comments, "So that's why you don't have time for Rodney."

Vicky chuckles answers, "It's not like that but I am thinking about it."

Antonio looks at her, "Are you joking? As many times as, he fucked you over how could you even be thinking about it?"

"He's KJ's father and he wants to be there for him. I know he feels bad because he wasn't there for Jordan and doesn't want the same thing to happen with KJ, we both want that."

Shea asks, "Are you thinking about it because you have feelings for him or so he can make up for lost time with KJ?"

Vicky takes a deep breath answers, I still do have some feelings for him he was my first and they say you never get over your first. He says he has some money saved up and will help out once he gets out."

Antonio hears this and shakes his head back and forth slowly, in a patronizing tone, "Wow some people never learn. I told you if you need a job I can put you up. Hell, you could be doing this instead of me."

Vicky irritated by his condescending tone spouts off," I don't have to justify myself to you. I'm a grown woman you live your life and I'll live mine."

Antonio looks at her again from the computer, "I'm sorry if I offended you but I've seen him dogg you out too many times but your right it's your life, just don't come crying to me if he does it again." He goes back to typing on the computer.

Shea responds to all this with, "I just want you to be happy. I don't care if it's with Keith………. or Rodney." They both start laughing.

"A couple of questions, when's he getting out? And have you told the kids?"

Vicky, "In about three weeks, and no I haven't told the kids. I'm telling them after school today."

Antonio without looking up from the computer, "It should be really fun to see how KJ takes the news."

She ignores his comment continues," If they have issues with it then it's a done deal it's not going to happen."

Shea is quiet for a moment finally says, "That's probably best you don't need to have any more drama in your life."

Vicky sits up on the couch starts putting on her shoes, "I need to get going I want to make sure I'm home when the kids get out of school."

Shea gets up from behind the desk and walks over to her and they hug.

Antonio looks up, "What's up with that meeting you and KJ are supposed to have with that boy's dad?"

She answers as she walks to the door, "He hasn't gotten back with me yet."

"Get with me when he does and I will try my best to be there."

Vicky nods her head and shuts the door.

14

VICKY, KJ, AND ERICKA ARE AT THE

dinner table, they are having canned beef stew and cornbread. Ericka sits down at the table asks excitedly, "Did you get the job?"

"I don't know I just interviewed today. It will probably be a couple of days before I know anything."

"I'm not worried I know you got it."

She looks at KJ who's eating his bowl of stew asks him, "How was your day?"

He answers calmly "Cool."

"This morning if you remember I said I wanted to talk to you?"

Both look at her now and shake their head in agreement, she takes a deep breath, "Well Keith has been calling me from prison and he is wanting to get back together. I told him I would have to talk to y'all before I decided anything."

Ericka, "When is he getting out?"

"In about three weeks, what are you feeling?"

Ericka "I don't know if you want him too I don't care."

KJ answers angrily, "Why's he coming back now? Where was he when Jordan was killed?"

"Take it easy KJ. You know he was in jail he couldn't be here."

He angrily answers back, "He wants to come back now and think everything is going to be alright? I hate him!!"

He gets up and walks away from the table.

Ericka, "Why does he always run away from the dinner table?"

She looks at Ericka and answers, "That's the only way he knows how to deal with his problems. I will give him some time to cool down."

Her phone alarm buzzes, she knows it's the timer to remind her to take her Effexor XR medication. She gets up walks to the counter pulls the bottle out of her tote. She turns off the alarm and sees that there is a text on it from Omar, *Good evening this is Mr. Russell, I'm checking to find out if we could meet to fix this situation between our boys.*

She takes two pills and walks back to the table to drink some tea with the medication.

She calls Antonio, he and Shea are lying in the bed watching tv. There is some Lifetime movie she is watching as he is dozing off. His phone rings, on the nightstand right next to him he ignores it. The phone progressively gets louder irritating her as she is watching the movie.

"Aren't you going to answer it?"

Antonio lying there with his eyes close, answers, "If it is important they'll call back."

The phone stops ringing she then asks, "So you don't care who it was?"

"Look it stop ringing watch your movie, let me sleep."

He's lying flat on his back she climbs over him to reach for the phone.

He feels her on top straddling him, his eyes open, and he looks up at her. She looks down at him and smiles. He smiles back, "That's what's up."

She laughs, "Not tonight darling, My monthly friend is in town,"

He responds sarcastically, "Of course she is."

She grabs his phone looks at it, "Vicky called."

She starts grinding on him, "What are you doing?" he asks incredulously.

She leans down and whispers in his right ear, "I like teasing you."

He playfully pushes her off, "That ain't cool. Give me my phone."

He snatches it from her left hand. She just rolls over away from him and starts laughing.

"Just because you're down this week doesn't mean you can't take care of me."

Still laughing she answers, "Umm yes it does, You don't get off unless I get off."

He smirks at her, looks at his phone, and calls Vicky, she is still sitting at the table, *"What's up?"*

"The boy's father who KJ was going to shoot just texted me wanting to meet up."

"What did you tell him?"

"I haven't got back to him I wanted to get with you before I answered. I want to do something this week and I know we have to do it after school. You got anything planned tomorrow around 4."

"No, I can make it Shea will be there."

"Ok, I will set it up for Friday at four. I will text you to let you know if it's on."

"Bet. Later." He hangs up.

She is surprised by his quick hang-up. She texts Omar *Yes, we need to meet. How bout tomorrow at four at my house?"*

She puts her phone down and finishes up her stew, she looks around and sees Ericka has left, she is there by herself.

After five minutes she gets a text from Omar, *That will work just text me your address, we will be there at four.*

She looks at her phone thinks, *Now to tell him. She gets up from the table walks to his room.*

15

THE DOOR IS SHUT SHE just goes straight into his room without knocking.

KJ's sitting at his desk reading the book, *The Boys Who Challenged Hitler Knud Peterson and The Churchill Club.*

"Is that homework?" she asks.

"I got a book report due after Christmas break."

She steps into the room and sits on the corner of the desk. "There are a few things that I want to talk to you about."

KJ puts a bookmark in the book and closes it. He looks up at her.

She continues, "I know you have some strong feelings about your dad especially concerning Jordan. It was not his fault, he didn't pull the trigger he wasn't even in town. Holding this against him is kinda unfair, don't you think?"

"When you say it like that yeah, but if he had been there maybe it never would have happened."

She shakes her head no, "We can play the maybe game a thousand different ways, but the reality is Jordan's dead and we have to accept it. She looks him in his eyes and continues. "Keith is your dad and I hope you will give him a chance."

He looks back at her and does a slight smile shrugs his shoulders responds," Okay."

"If there are any problems, he will be gone. You and Ericka will always come first. Now next thing, I just finished texting Mr. Russell and we are getting together Friday to get this thing between you and Dre settled."

"Do we have to?"

"It's a done deal. Why don't you want to do this?"

"I don't like that fool, don't trust him."

"Maybe if you got to know him you would see that he's not that bad."

KJ simply answers, "Maybe."

"Well, it's happening after school Friday, I will pick you up and we will meet here at the house your Uncle Antonio will be there which reminds me I need to text him to let him know it's on." She stands up and tells him, "Come back to the table and finish your dinner. You can bring your book. I've got to text your Uncle."

He gets up and grabs his book, she goes to the counter gets on her phone, and starts texting.

It's 2:55 Friday the last day of school before the Christmas break, Vicky's parked in front of the school waiting for KJ to come out. She hits the phone button on her steering wheel calls Omar after four rings,

Omar *"Hello?"*

Hello, I'm just checking to make sure everything is still on for today.

Omar, *"Of course. I'm on my way to get Dez right now about 10 minutes out."*

"I'm already here at the school." She sees students coming out of the building looks at her car clock it's 3:00. *"Well, they are coming out right now."*

"I will probably be a few minutes late but we will be there."

"No problem, I will text you my address after we hang up."

"Cool, See you later." He hangs up.

She takes the phone from the holder and begins to text him.

KJ comes and opens the front door. He jumps in the car puts his backpack in the backseat behind her asks, "Is it cool if we give Dre a ride home?"

She finishes texting and puts her phone back in its holder "Sure it's on our way."

He opens the door and waves for Dre to come on he jogs over to the car and opens the door behind KJ he gets in.

"Hello, Mrs. Skyy."

"How you doing Dre? I see your nose has healed?"

She starts the car and takes off, driving down the winding road leading off-campus she tells KJ, "I just spoke with Dez's father and we are still on. You ready?"

He shrugs his shoulders, "I guess."

She looks in her rearview mirror at Dre, tells him, "I'm glad to see that you and KJ are cool with each other again."

Dre smiles and tells her "Yeah we're good it was just a misunderstanding. Y'all meeting up with Dez? Is that a good idea?"

KJ answers, "I don't think so, but she is making me."

She looks back at Dre through the rearview mirror, "I can see why you would be skeptical, considering what he did to you. It was his father's idea and we need to try something."

Dre is quiet for the rest of the ride. They pull up to his house the next street over from KJ's.

He gets out of the car, "Thanks for the ride, Mrs. Skyy." He shuts the door, looking at KJ, "Let me know how it goes." KJ nods his head.

Vicky backs up, looks at the clock on her radio it's 330 tells KJ "I'm going to the store to get something to drink."

KJ "Can you drop me off?"

"Do you mind going with me to help me carry some of the bags?"

He sighs, "Okay."

It's 3:55 when they get back home after picking up a six-pack of sweet tea and some potato chips.

KJ carries the bags into the house and puts them in the kitchen.

He grabs his book goes to the couch and realizes Ericka is not there, "Where is Ericka?"

Vicky sits down beside him and starts working on her puzzle, "I didn't want her here for this, she's down at Zoey's house."

Vicky takes a deep breath looks at her phone the time is 409 she takes another deep breath, "Well he said he was running late."

She goes back to working on her puzzle, when she hears a vehicle pullup in their driveway, she gets up peeks out of the window sees a gray F150 parked behind her car.

"They're here."

16

SHE GOES BACK TO THE COUCH not wanting to appear edgy. She looks over at KJ, "You okay?" Still reading his book he shrugs his shoulder, calmly responds, "I'm good."

The doorbell rings, she gets up and answers it. Omar and Dez are on the porch standing next to each other.

She opens the door a little wider and gestures with her right hand for them to come in. "Hello, and welcome," she says in a cheerful voice.

Omar steps aside so Dez can go in first, as he follows behind he responds, "Thank you."

As they walk in KJ places the book on the coffee table on top of Vicky's puzzle and stares at Dez.

Vicky sees this and gestures for him to take a seat beside KJ. He walks over and sits on the opposite end of the couch. Omar walks in and Vicky tells him, "Sit here," pointing to the love seat.

He takes a seat, and she sits down beside him, he leans up from the loveseat, "To get the introductions out of the way, I'm Omar and that's my son Dezera."

Vicky looks over at Dez and nods at him she replies, "Nice to meet both of you."

KJ doesn't look at Dez, he does the what's up head bob to Omar.

Vicky, "Well this is my son KJ and I'm Vicky."

Omar does the same what's up head bob back to KJ.

Vicky looks at Omar, "What were you thinking we could do about this situation?"

"First I would like to thank you for responding to my text. I know it must have been tough under the circumstances of how we know each other."

She answers back, "I will confess I was a little suspicious when you reached out but I also know that something has to change before someone else dies." She looks at both KJ and Dez.

The doorbell rings again and she gets up, "That's probably my brother Antonio, I hope you don't mind I invited him over."

She opens the door, and Antonio immediately walks in, "Sorry about being late, got caught up with a client."

Omar stands up as Antonio comes into the house, "Tonio, Peppers." he extends his fist out for a fist bump.

Omar fits bump him "Omar Russell and that's my boy Dezera."

Vicky walks to the kitchen, "I'm going to get some chips and drinks."

Antonio looks around sees there are no seats, "Let me get a chair from the kitchen."

He walks to the kitchen in front of her and grabs a chair.

Sitting down he asks, "What did I miss?"

Vicky walks in with a big bowl of chips and a six-pack of bottled tea replies "You didn't miss anything we had just started. We were talking about what we could do to stop these two from killing each other."

"Can I make a suggestion?" Antonio asks.

Vicky and Omar both surprised by the question look at each other.

"Go ahead" he answers.

"You know the saying keep your friends close but keep your enemy closer, what if they hung out together for a day to get to know each other."

KJ hears this and exclaims, "Like a play date?"

"Not really but if that's what you want to call it."

Dezera shakes his head mumbles "That ain't happening I'm telling you that now."

Omar, "Boy don't tell me what you ain't gonna do."

Vicky looking at both of them watching the tension between them asks, "You see how they're reacting? You think we can trust them?"

Antonio, "All four of us can hang out one day."

"And do what?" KJ inquires.

Antonio at a loss for words after a few seconds, "Ummm go to my gym maybe workout, play some ball. Maybe go to that Playday place and check out a movie."

Omar tapping his left leg answers, "I can't be doing too much with this leg but I'll still hang out."

"Who knows maybe working out will help your leg."

Omar takes a deep breath, "We'll see." He looks over at Dez asks, "So what you think?"

"I already told you what I thought ain't nothing change."

KJ volunteers "I ain't cool with it either."

Vicky looks at him, "What harm could it do?"

Omar looks at both KJ and Dez, "Can y'all shake hands and come to a cease-fire, you know you keep your distance and I will keep my distance sort of thing."

Vicky shakes her head in agreement, urges KJ, "Go ahead."

He turns and looks at Dez who is looking at his father, "Are you serious?"

Omar answers, "Like a heart attack."

He slowly turns towards KJ and puts out his fist, KJ just stares down at it, Vicky, "What you waiting for?"

He does a light fist bump puts his head down and picks up his book.

Antonio, "Cool, it's a start."

Omar turns and looks at Vicky, "There is something I need to say before we go. I want to apologize for my son taking your son's life. I know this doesn't change anything but I wanted you to hear it from me personally."

Vicky a little choked up takes a deep breath, "Thank you I know that was difficult and I appreciate you having the courage to apologize in front of everybody."

Omar, "There is one more thing, I visited Dejuan a few weeks ago and he wanted me to ask would you and KJ come visit him?"

Shocked by the question a blank expression comes over her face she stares off into space. KJ hears the question and immediately gets up yells "Hell No!" as he walks past Antonio and his mom and goes out the front door.

Vicky finally stammers out, "I don't know give me some time to think about it."

Antonio seeing the emotion of the situation tells Omar, "Maybe it's best if y'all go."

Both Omar and Dezera stand up and walk to the door he comments, "Look I wasn't trying to cause any issues."

Antonio gets up and walks them to the door while Vicky still sits there stunned about what she was asked. He replies to Omar, "I know dogg, it just blindsided them. They'll be all right. Look I'll get your number from my sister and we will get together about the 'playdate.'"

Omar replies "Cool." Antonio opens the door and they leave.

17

ANTONIO OBSERVES KJ SITTING WITH his back turned away on the porch. He decides not to say anything and shuts the door.

She is sitting in the same spot with a blank look on her face. He walks over to her and puts his arm around her and asks, "Are you alright?"

"I think so, I just wasn't expecting my son's killer to want to talk to me. What do you think he wants?"

Antonio with a puzzled look on his face answers, "I don't know, we should've asked him before he left."

"What if he wants to taunt us about killing Jordan?"

"Why would he do that?"

"I don't know, just to torture us some more, to fuck with us. It's not like he was sorry when he was in court."

He comes back with, "I don't know that seems crazy. What if he wants to apologize? His father just did."

Vicky turns and looks at him with a bemused expression, "CRAZY?? Did you hear Reign in court? He is crazy. The way he stalked her after she broke it off with him and started going out with Jordan. That's the boy that pulled a gun on Jordan the night he got arrested. So, you believe it is crazy for him to want to fuck with us about killing Jordan. He is in prison for almost thirty years he doesn't have anything but time to fuck with us."

Antonio realizes this is a very sensitive subject, "That is all true but prison changes a man. With all that time maybe he has a change of heart and trying to make amends for his past actions."

Vicky looks away from him thinks for a few seconds, "Maybe. What do you think I should do?"

"I'm not sure both sides have some valid points, but I wouldn't just flat out say no. Maybe we should get KJ's thoughts on it, even though we both pretty much know how he feels."

"Can you go get him so we can talk to him?"

KJ is still sitting on the front porch. He opens the door and tells him, "Come in here, we want to talk to you."

He gets up and walks past Antonio and sits back in the same spot on the couch.

She looks at him and asks, "What are you thinking?"

In a defiant voice, he responds, "I ain't got nothing to say to him and I don't care what he wants to say to me." Vicky slowly shakes her head in agreement with him.

Antonio still standing up looks at both of them, "Before you shut it down get back with his dad, maybe he knows what he wants to talk to you about."

Vicky takes a deep breath reluctantly agrees, "Okay I will do that."

KJ angrily blurts out, "This nigga pops Jordan and would have popped me too if he hadn't run out of shells and you want me to go hear what he has to say?" Shakes his head, "No way bro." He then picks his book up off of the coffee table.

Antonio sees he cannot reason with KJ in his present mood so he lets it go.

He tells Vicky, "Well I gotta go, you got my number if you need it later." KJ does not look up from the book, just gives him the head bob.

Vicky stands up and hugs him, "I need to go get Ericka."

He walks out the door. She turns to KJ tells him, "Text Ericka and tell her I'm on my way."

Five minutes later she drives up and parks behind Reign's Camaro.

She does not feel like getting out of the car, her mind is still preoccupied with Omar's question, so she blows the horn.

Ericka runs out of the house with her metallic gold backpack and opens the car door and throws it in the back seat. She's in her usual joyous mood asks, "What's up momma?"

"Nothing much, did you get a chance to do your homework?"

Ericka answers, "There's no homework, this is the last day we got Christmas break."

She starts the car, puts it in reverse, and begins backing out. When she is at the end of the driveway. Reign comes out and is walking towards her car.

Vicky unexpectedly puts the car back in drive and pulls back up in the driveway. Ericka surprised by this inquires, "Momma what's wrong?"

She doesn't answer she pulls her car behind Reign's, she sees this and walks over to Vicky's car.

Vicky lets down the window. Reign asks, "Is there something wrong?"

"Do you have a few minutes? I would like to talk with you about something?"

Reign responds, "Sure what's up?"

"Well Dejuan's father came by the house to talk about the situation between KJ and Dez and he told me that he visited DJ and that he wants to talk to me and KJ and I don't know what I should do."

Reign asks, "What does he want to talk to you about?"

"I don't know I was so upset when he told me that I forgot to even ask."

"You know DJ has written me three or four times since he's been locked up it's funny I didn't even think he could write."

"What did his letters say?"

Reign with a hint of anger in her voice answers, "I don't know I didn't even open them, I tore them up and threw them away I didn't want to read anything from h m. I guess he got the message he hasn't written in about a month now."

Vicky chuckles a little, "You sound just like KJ right now."

"Are you going to visit him?"

She confesses, "I don't want to, but my brother wants me to think about it."

"Well I'm with KJ I don't want nothing to do with him, I might someday but right now I'm not ready. I know me and Jordan was just starting out but I believe we could have had something special and DJ took it away that night. I'm not sure if that helped but that's how I feel."

"Just talking to you helped, I'm not going to hold you up any longer I know you got someplace to be. Thanks."

Reign bends down and hugs Vicky through the window. She starts the car, Reign lets go she tells Vicky, "Let me know what you do," as she walks to her car. Vicky nods in acknowledgment as she lets up the window.

18

THAT NIGHT KJ'S READING IN THE KITCHEN while Vicky and Ericka are in the living room watching tv. He has been at it for the last hour, completely absorbed by the book.

His phone buzzes, he picks it up it is a text from Dre: *What happened with the meeting today?*

My mom and uncle want us to become best friends.

Dre: LOL. What's their plan?

KJ: Me and my Uncle, him and his dad are all supposed to hang out.

In the living room, Vicky's phone is ringing, she picks it up and walks to the kitchen, while it is still ringing she tells KJ "This is your father."

He puts his phone down with a confused look, she answers as she sits down beside him. Ericka being nosy follows behind Vicky and sits on the other side of KJ at the table.

After the prerecorded message plays Vicky in an easy tone responds, *"Good evening Keith."*

"What's up, baby? How is everything?"

"*It's okay I had a job interview a few days ago.*"

"*How did that go?*"

"*I felt good about it but I haven't heard anything back yet, hopefully soon. So how you doing?*"

"*Just counting down the days baby till we get back together. Have you talked with the kids about it?*"

"*It's funny you should mention 'the kids,' KJ is right here beside me. Do you want to talk to him?*"

Keith excitedly answers, "*Of course that's my boy put him on.*"

KJ reading his book does not take the phone, Vicky, "Your dad wants to talk to you."

He finally unwillingly takes the phone.

Keith in an excited voice, "*What's up KJ?*"

He responds in a solemn tone, "*Nothing much.*"

"*It's been a minute since we last talked. You ready for me to come back?*"

He answers in the same solemn tone, "I guess."

Keith noticing the tone asks, "*Are you salty about something?*"

He blurts out, "*If you would have been here Jordan wouldn't be dead.*"

Keith yells, "*You don't think I wanted to be there? He was my firstborn. I'm in prison, they don't let you out because someone dies. I get it from your mama now I'm getting it from you. If I could have been there I would have! Put your momma back on the phone."*

He gives the phone back to Vicky. He picks up his book and continues reading.

Keith still angry, *"That's fucked up! You blindsiding me like that."*

"What are you talking about? I didn't know he was going to come at you like that!"

"When you put him on I assumed you had everything straight."

She answers, *"Well Ericka is fine with it, KJ is still a work in progress, we talked and he is willing to give it a shot."*

Keith dismissively answers, *"Yeah, whatever. I'm getting out in two weeks. I got to go."* He hangs up.

Vicky puts her phone down, mumbles, "And he wants to get back together."

KJ puts his book down angrily asks, "Why did you do that mom?"

She feints innocence, "Do what?"

"You know what you did. I told you I didn't want to talk to him."

"I wanted y'all to talk so hopefully we could get everything out in the open, and get it settled."

"I told you I would give it a try you didn't have to do that."

She sheepishly answers, "Sorry."

KJ grabs his book and phone and goes to his room.

Ericka shakes her head, "There he goes again," she looks at her mother, "That was wrong…. but funny," and they both laugh.

The next morning Vicky's in front of the computer on the couch scrolling through Indeed looking for any leads she is frustrated that she hasn't heard anything back from her interview.

The kids are in their rooms doing their thing.

Her alarm goes off on her phone, she picks it up t's 10 am underneath is the message *Probation meeting at 11.*

Looking at it she thinks *Damn I almost forgot about it.*

She shuts the computer and yells, "KJ! Ericka! Put some clothes on KJ has a meeting with his probation officer in an hour."

He busts out of his room, yells, Today?!"

"Yes! Get dressed. We have to be there in an hour."

Ericka asks, "Do I have to go?"

"Of course, you can't stay here by yourself. Both of you get dressed we need to be leaving in 30 minutes."

All three of them are in the car with KJ in the front seat and Ericka in the back looking at her phone.

"How long do I have to keep coming to these check in's?"

"About another two months. At least they're getting shorter we've been getting in and out in about 15 minutes."

"Why do we have to even come if it's going to be so quick?"

"I don't know I guess making sure that you're staying out of trouble, it's your fault if you wouldn't got into that fight we wouldn't be here now"

This shuts him down and he just sits there quietly.

Ericka notices the uncomfortable silence asks, "Can we go Christmas shopping after were finish?"

Vicky was dreading this question takes a deep breath answers, "I am sorry but because I lost my job we don't have too much to spend on Christmas this year."

Ericka in a solemn tone responds, "Oh ok," and goes back to playing on her phone.

Vicky notices the tone looks in the rearview mirror, "I promise you will have some presents under the tree."

Ericka looks up from her phone and smiles at her.

She turns into the parking lot of the Allen County Juvenile Detention. "Remember don't say anything about what happened between KJ and Dez, they don't need to know."

She pulls into the parking lot and parks in front of the building she checks the clock it's 1050.

"Good timing."

KJ and Ericka go and take a seat under the clock on the other side of the door.

Vicky goes to the front desk to check in. She goes to sit down and just as she sits down, Mr. White comes out, in a friendly voice, "Come on back."

They all three get up and walk back following Mr. White he takes them to the same conference room and same circular table that KJ and Vicky first met with him.

As they all take a seat, Mr. White looks over at Ericka, "Who is this young lady."

Vicky answers," That's my youngest daughter Ericka I hope you don't mind if she came, with school being out I couldn't leave her at home."

He extends his hand to shake her's "Of course not, she's family."

He then turns towards KJ asks, "How's it going, young man?"

"Cool."

Mr. White shakes his head answers, "Talkative as ever I see," he turns towards Vicky, "How is everything at home?"

"It's been hectic I recently lost my job, and having a difficult time finding a new one. KJ has really stepped up during this time he has not had any problems at school or home. I really think he has made a change for the better."

KJ hears this and starts to smile, it makes him feel good to hear his mother give him a compliment.

Mr. White nods his head approvingly, comments, "It looks like you may be turning the corner. So, have you seen Dez or Dre?"

"I see Dez at school sometimes, but he doesn't always come. He does his thing I do mine, I see Dre more but he doesn't want to get in trouble and neither do I so we keep our distance."

"Sounds like everything is coming along pretty good with you" he looks at Vicky continues, "Except for your job situation. You got any good leads?"

"I went on an interview last week hopefully, I should be hearing something back soon."

He looks at Ericka, "You got anything to add?" His phone rings he looks at it, then turns it over.

Ericka looks up from her phone says, "I'm ready to go."

He chuckles, "The way it sounds everything is good so there is no reason to keep you. Maybe next time we can do this over the phone."

KJ, "Cool."

Everybody stands up he looks at Vicky, "Is it okay if you show yourselves out? I need to return this phone call."

"I understand." She answers as they all walk out.

In the car, Ericka, "So what are we going to do when we get home?"

"I need to get on the computer and do some more job hunting. You and KJ can do whatever."

As soon as she gets those words out, she gets a text message, *This is Ms. Sunny Givens from St. Anthony this message is to inform you that you are no longer being considered for the position of registered nurse. Thank you for your interest.*

She shakes her head in frustration, mumbles in a low tone, "This is turning into the worst Christmas of my life."

19

AS SHE DRIVES HOME, she gets that anxious feeling in her stomach. Her anxiety is starting up.

She spots a Quick Stop gas station coming up on the right. She turns into it and comments, "I need to get some gas." As she pulls into the pump she gets out to pay, Ericka yells out, "Can you get me a Code Red.

KJ's playing a game on his phone, "Get me one too."

Walking to the store she thinks, *They don't have a clue about money. We were just talking about it now they asking for some pop.* She walks into the store and goes to the drink cooler gets the two Code Reds and a bottle of water. She goes to the register and pulls out her debit card, "I need ten dollars on pump six."

After she gets back to the car she opens the front door drops the drinks on KJ's lap.

While the gas is pumping, she is looking through her tote for her medication. Rummaging through it thinks *Damn it on the counter.*

She opens the water takes a sip and does a breathing exercise, inhales a deep breath holds it a few seconds then exhales counting down from 10 after each breath till she gets to one.

The pump pings, she places the nozzle back up and leans on the driver's door for a few more seconds to get herself together.

She starts the car asks, "Who wants to go over to Shea's house?"

Ericka excitedly yells, "I do, she's my favorite aunt!"

KJ mumbles, "We know. You say it every time."

Vicky takes off from the gas station and gets on the phone, Shea immediately answers after two rings. Shea *"What's up girl?"*

"What you doing?"

"Not too much there's a Hallmark Christmas movie on. Me, and Mayla's watching, Gayla's on the computer filling out some college applications."

"Is it okay if me and the kids come by?"

"Yeah, your always welcome."

"We should be there in 15 minutes."

"Alright we'll see you then. Bye."

Fifteen minutes later they are pulling into the Camden Hills subdivision.

KJ looks around at all the $200,00 and up houses wistfully, says "Someday I'm going to live in a house just like these."

Ericka sarcastically answers, "Yeah, right."

They pull into the driveway and park behind Antonio's corvette.

They get out and ring the doorbell Shea answers, as soon as she opens it Ericka hugs her around the waist, tells her "You my favorite Aunt."

KJ hears this and slowly shakes his head. Shea then hugs Vicky and KJ. "Come in."

They walk in and sitting on the black leather couch are the twins Mayla and Gayla. They are on opposite ends, Mayla is looking at videos on her phone and Gayla is working on her laptop. Shea was sitting in the matching love seat facing the 70" flat screen hung on the wall. To the right is a 12-foot tall Spruce Pine Christmas tree done in a green and gold color scheme with presents underneath wrapped in the same colors.

Ericka sees the Christmas tree and is awestruck by it. "Wow, that's a big tree. We don't even have a tree."

KJ looks around and sees all the women in the room mumbles, "Great."

Mayla asks, "Ericka you wanna watch some Tik-Tok videos with me?"

Ericka runs over and plops down on the couch beside her.

Shea sees KJ's disappointment "You can play your Uncles Xbox if you like.

The controller is in the entertainment center underneath the tv."

He runs up and opens up the black entertainment center and pulls out a black controller and sits on the recliner.

Vicky sees that the kids are busy, "Can we go somewhere and talk?"

"Yeah sure," she motions with her head and walks to a door to the left side of the couch where Ericka and Mayla are sitting. Vicky follows behind her, inside is an office.

"This is the home office." She turns on a light. Vicky sits on a small blue couch and Shea sits beside her.

Shea looks at her, "I could hear it in your voice on the phone something is wrong. What's going on?"

"I didn't get the job. I just got the text about 10 minutes before I called you."

She continues with emotion in her voice, "They didn't have the compassion to call and tell me in person."

Shea shakes her head, responds, "That's just wrong. I know how much you were counting on that job."

Vicky looks at a small Christmas tree on Antonio's desk. "It is so hard to have the Christmas spirit when it seems like everything is working against you."

"Is that why you haven't put up a tree yet?"

"This will be our first Christmas without Jordan. I don't have a job. KJ almost killed a boy. If this was your life would you be in a Christmas spirit?"

Shea grabs her hand, looks at her, in an upbeat tone tells her, "Stop looking at the negative, Christmas is a time to celebrate what you have. Not what you don't, KJ is doing better right? Keith is about to be released and y'all getting back together, that's something to look forward to."

Vicky shakes her head, Shea continues, "That is not the only job out there you know... our offer is still available."

Vicky eagerly answers, "I'll take it. That is one of the reasons I can by to make sure it's still good."

"I'll call Antonio to let him know we have a new employee. When do you want to start?"

"What about after Christmas?"

"Okay, What about after the New Year. What are your plans for Christmas?"

"I haven't made any."

"Why don't y'all come over, we spent Thanksgiving at your house, come here for Christmas. We will make sure the kids have some presents under the tree. I know you said that you're not in the Christmas spirit, but there ain't no reasons the kids can't have a good Christmas."

Vicky laughing answers, "Okay, I don't want to be the Grinch who stole Christmas."

20

CHRISTMAS DAY!! VICKY AND the kids are in the car at the usual spots.

As she starts the car on the way to Shea's house she announces, "We are going to see Jordan today." "Why? It's Christmas." KJ exclaims.

"That's exactly the reason why we're going today. Now is a perfect day, we can see him for a few minutes he is still part of the family."

KJ whining, "How long we going to be there?"

Vicky now annoyed by his attitude and questions answers, "Until we leave."

He takes a deep breath and starts sulking not even attempting to hide his disgust.

As she driving she looks over at him, "So this is the attitude you're going to have for Christmas? Shaking her head ask, "Where did I go wrong with you?"

Ericka, "After we leave we still going to Aunt's Shea's?"

"Of course, and your Aunt Michelle and your cousins will be there and it will be like a normal Christmas."

Smiling she sits back and answers, "Cool."

At the cemetery, Jordan's gravesite is about 20 yards from a big pecan tree. Vicky remembers it from the funeral. She drives slowly down the single one-lane road till she sees the tree.

She pulls to the side of the road and parks. "We're here."

She and Ericka start to unbuckle their seatbelt, she looks at KJ who is just sitting there "I'm not going," he says.

She dismissively responds, "Whatever, let's go Ericka."

They both get out of the car, she walks around and takes Ericka's hand tells her, "Follow me and don't walk over anybody's grave it is disrespectful to the dead." Ericka shakes her head in response.

Vicky starts walking with her head down looking for Jordan's grave.

After wandering around for about 10 minutes she finally locates it, it looks different from what she remembers, from the funeral.

She lets go of Ericka's hand kneels down and lightly rubs her hand over the headstone, she whispers his name reading it *Jordan Vincent Skyy*

December 11, 2002 – March 24, 2018, underneath is the quote she put on to express her emotions, *You Never Said Goodbye.*

Tears start to form in her eyes as she continues to run her hands over the letters whispers "I miss you so much, I love you this is not how it was supposed to be, they say the Lord works in mysterious ways, but this is the biggest mystery of my life. I just wanted to come see you since we didn't get a chance on your birthday. We can't stay too long we have to get to Aunt Shea's for Christmas I just needed to stop by to say you're not forgotten and I love you. She gets up and walks away with her head still down, tells Ericka, "If you want to say something I will give you your space."

Ericka standing there has a puzzled look on her face asks, "What should I say?"

Vicky her eyes still watery answers, "I don't know sweetie, say what you feel."

She looks down at his headstone, "I don't know what to say. After a few seconds pause, "Love you big bro," kisses her two fingers, and touches his headstone. Turns around and walks to Vicky.

As they get in the car Vicky buckles her seatbelt locks at KJ, "Are you sure you don't want to visit him? We are the only ones here, it might help you find peace... closure."

KJ, "Closure?"

"My doctor told me I needed closure to get over Jordan's death and I know that you do too."

"Whatever, but I'll go since we are here."

"Good."

He gets out and walks straight to Jordan's tombstone. He stands over it and looks down at it, "Damn why did he kill you? I wanna do his brother so bad so he can see how it feels. I promised you and mama I wasn't going to do nothing. Now his dad comes over to our house wanting us to be best friends. What the fuck is that about? I'm not going to do anything to him, but if he comes at me he is going to be dealt with. We ain't never going to be boys I don't care what they say. Then he tells us that DJ wants to talk to us. What's he got to say to us? I don't know or care he ain't saying nothing that I want to hear." Well that's about it bro, mom said talking to you might make me feel better, I think she was right. J I gotta go bro good talkin with you."

Back at the car Vicky, "You okay?"

"Yeah I'm good I think it helped."

She smiles and starts the car, "Let's go have a Merry Christmas."

21

OMAR AND DEZ ARRIVE AT Orange Coral, there is a line to get in, Dez surprised, "I guess a lot of people are having a miserable Christmas."

Omar doesn't respond, he pulls his phone off his hip holster and checks the time, "We got about 15 minutes before they come. Will just get our plates and wait for them to come."

Dez, "Who's them?"

"Crystal, she has two kids."

"Kids? Where did you meet her?"

"At work, we work on the line together. We started talking and found out that neither of us had plans so we decided to get together for Christmas here at Orange Corral, so our families can meet."

They get in line and it snakes out to the entrance door. After a tedious ten-minute wait, they finally make it to the register. Dez who is in front of Omar grabs his tray and goes to the banquet line. He thinks *I didn't get anything for Christmas I'm chowing down.*

He loads up on the fried chicken, macaroni and cheese, string beans, catfish, buttered rolls. Omar stops at a table and puts the drinks down and his phone and slowly walks over to get his food.

Just as he, makes it to the buffet line, he hears, "Omar Omar, we here."

Dez walking back to the table hears this looks up and there is a thick black woman about 5'6" she is brown-skinned with long cornrow braids that come down to her waist. She has on some smoky gray eye shadow, and dark cherry red lipstick, with oversized hoop earrings. Right beside her are two kids one boy and one girl. He walks right to the table and sits down.

Omar walks back to the table and drops his plate off.

Dez sits there and begins to eat, Omar walks over and pays for Crystal.

They walk over to the table, the youngest kid a boy about six years old is running around them in circles. The other kid a girl about nine calmly walks beside her mom.

They arrive at the table Omar starts the introductions, "Crystal this is my son Dezera," he looks up from his plate and smiles slightly at her.

"Well, Dezera these are my two kids, McKenzie, pointing at the girl and Tariq" pointing at the boy. He is right beside Dez and points at the macaroni and cheese, "You gonna eat that?"

Dez annoyed by his questioning simply shakes his head yes.

She looks at Dez, "I know we just met but could you do me a big favor and watch Tariq while we go get our plates."

Dez meekly answers, "Sure."

All three walk to the banquet line. The boy then sits down beside him and is pointing at different things on his plate asking, "Are you going to eat that?" After about the third item, Dez tries to ignore him, he shakes his head, thinks *Damn this kid is annoying.*

Omar's phone starts to ring in front of him and he can see it's from Wallace/Ware prison. He yells to his father, "Pops, your phone's ringing, I think it's Dejuan."

He yells, "Well answer it damn it." Dezera answers it and hears the prison recording after it Dejuan happily shouts out "Merry Christmas Pops"

"Bro DJ it's me Dez."

DJ surprised asks, "Where's Pops? Everything all right?"

"Yeah, he's fine. Were at Orange Corral and he is getting a plate."

"How was your Christmas?"

"This is it right here. We here at Orange Corral with his new girlfriend. "

Omar arrives at the table snatches the phone, "Give me that, he doesn't have a lot of time."

He puts the phone to his ear, as DJ asks, "How does she look? Is she fine?"

Omar, "Who you talking about?" He then figures it out jokes with him, "You don't need to worry about that, you need to make sure you don't drop the soap."

He walks away from the table and goes outside to get some privacy, "*Very funny pops. Merry Christmas.*"

"Merry Christmas son I'm surprised to hear from you today."

"They gave everybody a 10-minute phone call for Christmas. Dez says y'all eating out."

"We having a Christmas dinner with a friend and her kids."

"What's her name?"

"Crystal, we work together at the plant, she has two kids Were all here together getting to know each other, nothing serious."

"That's what's up. When you coming to visit again?

"I'm not sure it will have to be some time after New Year's".

"Did you tell Jordan's family that I want to talk to them?"

He is hesitant now, *"Yeah I told them it didn't go too well, both the mom and boy kinda freaked out. She started crying and he walked out of the room pissed off. They both were pretty messed up they asked me to leave and I never got an answer."*

"Can you call and ask if they would come, it's really important."

"I will text her next week to ask her, based on how they reacted I can't promise you nothing."

"Cool, I got to go my times up."

Omar starts walking back into the restaurant going to the table, *"Alright son, be safe in there I will text her next week and let you know something when you call."*

He gets back to the table everybody, is sitting down and eating he looks at Crystal tells her, *"There is something I need to tell you."*

It's 9 pm, Vicky and KJ are back at home. Ericka is spending the night with Shea. Vicky's in the living room opening a puzzle she got for Christmas. KJ is in his room playing one of his new video games.

Her phone rings, in her tote, she reaches over and picks it up, she looks at the screen it's Keith.

After the prerecorded message, Keith says, *"What's up boo?"*

She is pleasantly surprised to receive this greeting based on their last conversation.

"Merry Christmas Keith. How you doing babe?"

"I'm good just chillin counting down till we can be together. How was your Christmas?"

"We went to visit Jordan's grave early in the day, then went over to Antonio and Shea's for Christmas dinner.

Ericka had a good time hanging with her cousins. KJ even had a nice time."

"Cool, nothing happened here pretty much just another day."

She interrupts him," *I need to apologize for the last time we talked, after I spoke with KJ I know that I was wrong to put y'all in that position."*

Keith quickly responds, "We good I'm over it. How does he feel about me moving in?"

"To be honest with you he is a little apprehensive but is willing to give it a shot."

"I respect that. Everything else going good?"

"I didn't get the job so I'm going to work with Antonio and Shea at their fitness place until something comes through."

"Antonio huh? I don't know what his beef is with me but he needs to man up if he got a problem."

"What are you talking about?"

"Don't worry about it. If there is an issue we'll work it out. Well I'm getting released in two weeks, and I got some cash stashed away to help out, so you won't be there long.

"Two weeks, do you know exactly what day and time?"

"No, I should be hearing something sometime next week."

"Alright then keep me posted."

22

THE HOLIDAY SEASON IS OVER both KJ and Ericka are back in school. Vicky pulls into the parking lot of Shea's and Antonio's fitness center. It's 8:30 am, there are five cars in the parking lot, she parks beside Shea's white BMW.

As she goes inside, Rodney is wiping down the counter, he stops when he sees her and comes from behind the counter, "Good morning Vicky good to see you again. What brings you here so bright and early?"

She is happily surprised that he remembers her name.

"Today is my first day at my new job. Are Antonio and Shea in the office?"

"Shea's back there, Ant hasn't made it in yet." Still smiling he asks" Would you like for me to show you back?"

"Thanks that's okay I remember."

"Just asking," as he walks back behind the counter and starts wiping it again.

As she walks by the workout equipment, she passes by two other employees a man and a woman she doesn't know they are wiping down some workout machines.

The office door is closed, she knocks on the door, Shea yells, "Come in."

Vicky opens the door, and Shea is sitting at the desk applying lipstick using her phone as a mirror. She walks in a takes a seat at the other desk putting her phone and purse down.

"What's up girl? You going on a date?"

Shea laughingly answers, "No girl I got a meeting with the bank for a loan. We're thinking about expanding."

"That's great!! Why didn't y'all say something?"

"Antonio wanted to keep it quiet until we know for sure it's going to happen."

"Where is he?"

"He wanted to make it to this meeting but he is not feeling well."

"It's not serious is it?"

"He believes it may be a virus, he knew this meeting was important so he wanted me to make it." She gets up from the desk and steps around it asks, "How do I look?"

She's wearing a loden green solid button-front dress suit with sandalwood color pumps. She does the model twirl to show it off.

Vicky checks her out, "You looking like fire girl, if I had your figure I would be showing it off too."

"Ain't no reason you can't, you work here you can use all of this stuff for free. We can work out together."

Shea grabs her clutch and walks out the door, Vicky follows behind her, "I don't know it's been a real long time since I've done anything."

Shea at a quick pace continues, "Think about it you got time. I gotta go I can't be late. She walks past the counter where Rodney is sitting typing on the computer.

Vicky stops at the counter leans on it, "What am I supposed to do while you're gone?"

She turns around smiling answers, "Hang out with Rodney he will show you around," she walks out the door.

She mumbles, "That bitch, this feels like a setup."

Rodney hearing this walks from behind the counter, "So where would you like to start?"

"I don't know, show me around."

Rodney walks closer to her, waves his right hand for her to follow him, as they walk into the main fitness room it is painted gray with mirrors on the walls to the left and right. The floor has a black foam-like surface covering it. The same man and woman are still wiping down the machine on the left side, Rodney calls them over he looks at Vicky, "Have you met them yet?"

"No, I sure haven't", she answers. They are both white in their late 20's early 30's wearing the red and black uniforms. As they approach, Rodney looks at them, "This is Lacy and Rody they're both personal trainers here." He continues, "This is Vicky this is her first day." They smile and shake her hand. "Well, we need to get back to wiping down the machines," Lacy says. Vicky and Rodney walk over towards the right he walks up to a machine, "This row of machines is for your cardio workout," as he slaps the seat of a Nordic track cycle, there are three of them. Next to them are three Nordic treadmills and finally 2 rowing machines. He continues walking and stops at the weight bench, "Here are the workout benches, we have three of them. He turns around looks at her, "You never did answer my question."

Vicky taken back, "What question is that?"

"Who is older?"

She chuckles, comes back with, "I'm not trying to be rude, but I don't want to talk about my personal life with someone I don't know."

"The only way we are going to get to know each other is by talking."

Vicky irritated, "I'm not sure if you are just making conversation, or something else, but I'm not interested in anything but my job."

"Gotcha, no problem."

He turns and walks towards a Bow flex weight machine. There are three of them right beside each other says to her, "These are our newest additions, you can do all kinds of exercises with these."

He looks at his watch, "I need to get upfront, we are about to open."

His attitude immediately changes in that he is a little cold to her. She thinks, *He seems like a nice man but I not trying to lead him on. I really want this to work with Keith this time.*

She realizes she is just standing there in the workout area by herself turns around and goes to the office. She takes a seat behind the computer mumbles to herself, "What am I supposed to do now? If I knew the password I would log on and at least look at some jobs."

She looks at the phone beside the computer, picks it up pushes the home button on the speed dial, mumbles, "I hope this is to his house," after five rings, Antonio answers the phone sounding weak, *"Shea, What's up?"*

"This is Vicky. You okay? You sound terrible."

"Can't lie I have been better what's up?"

"Shea's at that meeting and I'm just sitting in the office not doing anything and I wanted to log on to check out some other employment opportunities."

"Where's Rodney?"

"He's at the front counter. Why?

"Just hang out with him until Shea gets back."

"I'm not sure that's a good idea."

"What happened?"

"It's nothing really, just while he was showing me around he was asking me a lot of questions."

"A lot of questions? Like what kind of questions."

"Just some questions about me, I guess he was being friendly, Me and Keith are going to get back together when he gets out and I don't want to send Rodney any mixed signals."

"I would have been shocked if he was harassing you. I've known Rodney for about four years, he used to come work out before he got the job. He is a straight-up dude and he has been going through a lot in the last couple of years. His wife passed away about 2 years ago. He started hitting the bottle good to help him escape the pain."

Vicky inquires, "What brought him out of it?"

"His Faith and it was his kids having an intervention with him. He's better than your ex who you keep going back to."

"Look we already had that discussion. Can you give me the password so I can log on?"

Shea unexpectedly comes into the office Vicky a little surprised greets her, "What's up? How did it go?"

She walks over to the other desk and sits down answers, "Good really good."

"They were disappointed that you weren't there but they were very interested in our expansion ideas.

I got some forms that we need to look over in the next few weeks. They want to come and do a tour when you're feeling better."

"Hopefully this is just a 24-hour bug and I'll be back tomorrow."

Vicky's phone buzzes, she pulls it out of her purse it is a text from Omar, *I just wanted to reach out to you to see if you thought about going with me next time I go down to see DJ.*

23

VICKY SHOWS HER PHONE to Shea tells her, "He is asking about going to see his son again."

Antonio over the phone asks, *"What's going on?"* Shea puts him on speaker.

"That boy's father just texted me and asked if I could visit with his son? I really don't want to go especially since I don't know what he wants to say."

Antonio over the speaker, *"Why don't you call him?"*

Vicky picks up her phone and calls, the phone rings.

Omar answers, *"Hello?"*

"Omar, I got your text, I haven't given it too much thought but I know I can't keep avoiding it. I just need to know what does he want to talk about?"

"He wouldn't tell me he says he just has some things he needs to say and that he wants to tell only you and your son."

Antonio over the other phone loudly states, *"I'ma put it out there, we just need to know if he's playing some kind of twisted game where he is trying to mess with her about Jordan."*

Omar is caught off guard by Antonio, *"Who is this?"*

"This is her brother Antonio we met when you came by a few weeks ago."

"Alright bro no problem, I've been visiting my son for the last year and I know he is not playing any games with you. Even if I thought he was I would not be helping him, I know he is sorry we all are, I think he is just trying to make things right if that is possible."

Vicky's thrown off by that comment, "*Right?? You can never make it right unless he can bring back the dead.* She pauses a few seconds to regain her composure, "When are you going to see him again?"

"I' don't know. When would be a good time for you?"

"I don't have anything planned two weeks from now. I'm not saying yes but I will consider it, you saw my son's reaction, and ain't nothing changed with him."

"Hopefully you can talk with him because he really wants to talk with both of you. I got to get back to work let me know something."

"I will talk to KJ and get back with you later this week." She hangs up.

Antonio "*Well I'm out too, I'm feeling tired again. Keep me in the loop.*"

Shea looks at Vicky excitedly asks, "You going to go visit him?"

"I am thinking about it after talking with him. I would like KJ to come also but I know that's going to be a battle."

"If you think it's for the best don't give him a choice."

"That may be my only option. She changes the subject, "Tell me about the meeting?"

"It was great, I think we have a good chance to get this loan, they just want to meet with both of us and come check out the place. You know when we do expand we are going to need to hire more people…. maybe you ought to consider making a career change."

Vicky surprised by Shea's suggestion, "Girl I don't know nothing about working out."

"You are already a health care professional so it's not like you don't know anything. We got the staff to train you, I didn't know anything until Antonio showed me. We about to blow up you best get in now."

Vicky laughs, "Slow your roll, let's see how things work, it ain't always easy working with family."

Shea smiles answers, "Think about it."

Vicky is at home sitting on the couch, waiting for the kids to come home from school.

Ericka comes in and takes a seat beside her inquires in her normal upbeat mood, "How was your first day at work?"

She answers equally upbeat, "It was good, not really sure what I'm doing but it was a pretty good day. It's nice not to be dealing with entitled patients and drama all day"

"What is your job?"

"Today all I did was input some of their client information in the computer. I'm thinking about working with them full time."

"Bet."

KJ walks in yells "What's up?" He goes straight to the kitchen to the refrigerator.

She has decided to just tell him straight up about going to see Dejuan. She gets up off the couch, walks to the table stands behind a chair. "I spoke with Mr. Russell today at work and he asked about us going to visit Dejuan?"

He shuts the fridge door and looks at her, "What did you tell him?"

"I told him I would seriously think about it."

He responds in a defiant tone loudly, "You can go if you want but I ain't going."

He walks away, she comes up behind him and grabs his right arm and turns him around, "You not walking away this time. You can't keep running from this."

He yells "Why do I have to go if I don't want to?"

She yells back at him, "Aren't you tired of always being angry and pissed off? You got a chip on you shoulder about the size of Texas you're carrying around. If you faced him you can get some things out, and clear the air. You got too much anger and hate to be only 14."

KJ now breathing heavily with tears in his eyes, "You think this is just about Jordan getting popped? That nigga was going to do me if he hadn't run out of bullets. He had it pointed at my head and pulled the trigger, I will never forget hearing that click. Both me and Jordan would be dead. That nigga wanted to kill me and I'm just supposed to forgive and forget, ain't no way boy." He is slowly shaking his head tears rolling down his face.

Her hearing all this for the first time she realizes all the emotions he has been keeping bottled up all this time. She grabs him and pulls him in hugging and squeezing him, whispering in his right ear, "I'm so sorry I didn't realize how much this affected you. I'm so sorry. I'm so sorry." She repeats it over several times in his ear.

She lets go after about a minute.

She looks him in his eyes, "I talked with his dad, he says he believes he wants to apologize. Don't you want to be there if he does?"

He looks at her wiping the tears from his face answers, "If you want me to go I will, but not for him but for you."

"I don't want to force you but I believe this could help you heal."

He looks her in the face "I'll go," He turns and walks to his room.

24

LATER THAT NIGHT AT 9 PM as Vicky is preparing to take her shower her phone rings with the weekly phone call from Keith.

After the customary prerecorded message, Vicky excitedly asks, *"I'm glad you called so what day you getting out?"*

"That's what I wanted to talk to you about, you don't have to pick me up."

"Why?? You not getting out?"

He hesitantly answers, *"I've decided to get back with Madison."*

"Who the hell is Madison!?"

"She was the shorty I was with the night I got arrested?"

"You decided this now? What changed your mind?"

"After the talk with KJ, it made me think. Is this a good idea? He was cold towards the plan, so I hit up Madison as another option. She told me she just had a baby and it's mine."

"Baby??" She yells, *"How the hell you having a kid when you been locked up for the last 11 months?"*

"Well, we did smash a few times while we were down here. I don't know for sure if she's mine but the math adds up."

"Help me make sense of this, basically you've been begging to get back together for the last six months. I finally agree to it, then a week before it's supposed to happen you back out. That's a punk-ass move, Keith."

"I'm not trying to hurt you I thought you would be cool with it. I'm going to be in town I can still be there for KJ."

"That's not how it works, you can't be picking and choosing either you all in or not and you made your choice." She hangs up the phone. Her hands shake as she puts the phone down.

The next morning at the table KJ and Ericka are eating the cereal Lucky Charms.

Vicky comes into the kitchen, sits down at the table tells them "Keith is not coming."

Ericka looks up from her cereal bowl, "Why? What happened?"

Not wanting to have to explain everything she simply says," He just changed his mind." She looks at KJ, "What do you think?"

He shrugs his shoulder, "Sorry but not sorry, He's always capping."

Vicky is confused by his terms, "What does that mean?"

Ericka answers, "He's calling him a liar."

Vicky shakes her head in agreement. She gets up, "Alright let's get moving I need to get to work."

Both KJ and Ericka get up he inquires to Vicky, "How are you doing?"

"To be honest I am disappointed, we've been talking about getting together the last three months just for h m to back out when it was time. She sighs, "What's done is done let's go."

While walking to the car, she tells KJ as they into the car, "Just so you know I going to text Mr. Russell today to let him know where going with him next time he visits You still good?"

"No, but I said I would so we good."

She drops them off at school and heads to work.

Vicky turns into the parking lot to the fitness center just as she pulls into a spot, Shea pulls in and parks to the right of her.

Vicky's still thinking about Keith reneging on her, gets out of her car. Shea quickly gets out and yells, "Good morning."

"Good Morning, Shea."

Shea catches her down mood, "What's going on?"

They walk in together no one is at the front counter, as they walk past Vicky tells her "I talked with Keith last night…" Shea interrupts her as they walk into the workout area where Rody and Lacy are doing the morning wipe down of the fitness equipment. "Let's talk about it in the office."

As they walk by Shea turns towards them says cheerfully, "Good morning,"

they both pause and answer back, "Good morning."

Shea asks, "Have y'all heard from Rodney this morning?"

Rody answers, "He came in early and got a workout in, He went home to shower and change."

"Alright, Antonio should be here shortly." They continue walking to the office Shea unlocks it and they walk in. Vicky sits down on the couch while Shea goes behind the desk and starts logging in on the computer.

"You were saying?"

"Keith called last night, I'm thinking we're about to make plans for me to pick him up, instead he tells me he is getting back with that hoe."

"What hoe? What are you talking about?"

"When he got arrested he was with some hoe, Madison?"

"Do you know her?"

"No, that's not important, you know we've been planning to get together after he got out. A week before he gets out he ups and drops me. I was counting on him to help out."

Shea slowly shakes her head in disbelief, "Antonio did warn you."

She stares at Shea says, "That's not what I wanted to hear. I don't need to hear I told you so from you, I already know I'm get that from Antonio. Please don't say anything to him."

"Look at like this, now you don't have no excuse not to holla at Rodney. You know he is feeling you. He's a good man girl just getting back out there, you better get on him before someone does."

Vicky stands up, "I don't know, after I came off on him I wouldn't feel right."

"Don't worry about it I got this."

Antonio and Rodney walk into the office.

Vicky still standing looks at Antonio smiling she says, "I'm glad that you are feeling better."

He walks over to her and they hug, "Yeah, I'm not quite 100 percent but I'm much better."

He walks behind, the computer to Shea as she gets up.

Rodney smiles at Vicky but doesn't say anything locks at Antonio, "All right Ant I will get with you later." He turns around about to walk out.

Shea blurts out, "So Vicky you were talking about wanting to start working out, maybe you can come in early and meet up with Rodney."

Vicky caught off guard answers, "Yeah I'm not sure. I have to get my kids to school in the morning?"

"Girl I can come by and make sure they're dressed and fed. No problem."

Vicky looks at Rodney, "Would you be okay with me working out with you? I'm trying to lose a few pounds."

He stutters a minute surprised by the question, "Umm sure, I'm a personal trainer, and that's what trainers do. Do you have any certain goals in mind?"

"Well, I would like to lose twenty, twenty-five pounds and tone up overall."

I'll tell you what, why don't you come up to the front when you get the chance and we can work on a plan."

Smiling she answers, "Okay." He walks out and shuts the door.

Antonio now sitting behind the computer asks, "How did the talk with KJ go?"

She sits back down, takes a deep breath, "It was rough at first but as we talked I found out he is holding in a lot. Not just because Jordan was killed but that boy was gonna kill him. It messed with him a lot more inside than I understood."

Antonio sitting there says quietly, "Man that's heavy."

Shea standing beside Antonio mumbles, "Poor baby I couldn't even imagine."

"So, you're going to see him?" He gets up from the computer walks around the desk.

"Yeah, we both are I think it will be good for us." She grabs her phone and begins to text.

He tells Shea, "I'm going to check out some new equipment for the expansion. Do you want to come?"

"No. I'm good."

He opens the door, "Alright I will see you in a few hours."

Right after the door shuts Vicky asks, "What the hell was that about?"

"What?? I just hooked you up, your welcome."

Vicky giggles, "Thanks, I don't have anything to work out in."

Shea reaches into her purse and pulls out a credit card and gives it to Vicky "Get a couple of outfits."

She looks at Shea's hand, "Are you sure?"

"Of course, I'm ownership too it's a business expense."

She takes the credit card, "Great I will go shopping after the kids get out of school. Thanks for the hookup."

25

THE HORN SOUNDS OVER THE LOUDSPEAKER, Omar slowly limps off the line it's been a long tedious ten-hour shift. He is exhausted and ready to go home. He slowly follows behind some of his coworkers. He takes off his gloves and orange safety vest as he limps along. He smiles and does the head nod to some of the oncoming shift, as they pass by. Once he gets to the time clock there is a line of eight to ten people waiting.

After clocking out he steps off the floor goes to the back of the house and places his vest and gloves in his locker. He grabs his hoodie and backpack. In the parking lot, he sees Crystal waiting for him at his truck he is about 50 yards away. He reaches in his pocket for the clicker and unlocks it.

She hears the door unlock looks around and sees him limping along to the truck, she smiles and waves at him. He yells at her, "Go ahead and get in it's open."

She jumps in and is looking through her purse for her phone.

He struggles to get in the truck because his leg has stiffened up due to the cold weather.

"Damn I hate this weather this always happens when it gets cold."

He massages his knee for a few seconds, starts the truck

"I'm sorry I kept you waiting."

"I'm good I just appreciate you giving me a ride while my car is in the shop."

She takes her phone, "I need to let the sitter know I'm on my way to get

Tariq and McKenzie."

As she is talking on the phone he drives away, he checks his phone for messages.

The voicemail comes over the truck speakers from Vicky, "*Mr. Russell this is Vicky me and KJ, will go with you the next time you visit DJ. Get back to me when you can.*"

Crystal hearing this asks, "What is she talking about?"

"There is something I need to tell you."

She looks at him, "Okay, go ahead."

"I wasn't sure when would be a good time to tell you, but now works, my oldest son Dejuan is in prison for murder."

Her eyes widen, she stares at him shocked at a loss for words on what to say.

He comes to a stoplight, "You okay?"

"Umm, sure I didn't know what you were going to say but I didn't expect that."

"My boy Dejuan shot this other boy, Jordan over a girl."

Crystal in an excited voice exclaims, "That's it!! I need to know more than that! Was there a fight between them? Did the other boy have a gun too? Was the girl one of their girlfriend? Did she have anything to do with the shooting? You think you can drop a bomb like that and not give any details?"

He takes off from the light, chuckles to himself mumbles, "I've should have known it wasn't going to be that easy." He doesn't like to talk about it. "Between court and what he has told me it has to do with this girl Reign who broke up with him and started going out with Jordan. He and Jordan had an ongoing beef about it, they got into a fight and my son ended up shooting and killing him. He says he didn't mean to kill him just when they were fighting he got caught up in the emotion and shot him without even thinking about it. "

As he is driving she is silent absorbing everything he just told her. After a few more seconds, "Your son was jealous and killed this boy over his ex-girlfriend?"

Omar surprised with her point-blank assessment answers, "I guess when you put it like that…..yeah."

She looks at him, "If this doesn't work do I have to watch my back?"

He looks back at her, "You think if we break up you asking am I going to kill you?"

He comes to another stoplight and stares at her she stares back at him responds, "It's not like it's a stupid question, you told me you did time now you tell me your son is in jail for murder. What would you think?"

Her left hand is on the truck seat he reaches out and touches it with his right hand. "I did time for a totally different thing, I was a different person then. Mia my ex left us during the trial I know it just wasn't the trial we had other problems before the trial, that was just the last thing. It hurt me to my soul that she would leave but I knew it was for the best. If this doesn't work out, it wasn't meant to be. I'm not my son."

He takes off, she sits there quietly he asks, "Does this change anything?"

She looks out the window "I don't know I have to think about it."

Vicky comes home both KJ and Ericka are already there. Ericka's on the couch playing on her phone. KJ's in his room.

She's in an upbeat mood, as she walks in, announces loudly, "KJ come here. We're all going shopping I need some gear to work out in."

He comes into the living room looks at her, "You are going to work out?"

Both KJ and Ericka look at each other amused.

"Come on let's go." She waves her right hand signaling for them to get moving.

As they walk out the door she responds, "Why is it so hard to believe that I want to work out? I used to run track in school."

As they are getting in the car, he answers, "But that was a hundred years ago."

Ericka asks, "Why are you working out?"

"I was talking to your Aunt Shea and she talked me into it. It's a chance to get in shape and it's free, I figured why not give it a try."

She's driving down the road Ericka asks, "You and Aunt Shea are working out together?"

"No, I'm working out with a coworker. She is going to take y'all to school tomorrow."

Ericka, excitedly answers, "Cool She's my…"

KJ interrupts her yells "Favorite Aunt. We know."

"Are you doing this because of what happened with daddy?"

Vicky comes to a stoplight, "No I told you your Aunt Shea talked me into."

KJ mumbles "If you say so." He asks, "You gonna work out every day?"

She takes off from the light yells once more, "Hell no! Let's see how the first day goes."

Both KJ and Ericka laugh at her reaction.

"Where are we going?"

"To the Town Center to see what's there?"

They arrive, they walk into the Hoops and Hops store. Reign is at the register; the store is empty. She sees them come in and immediately heads over. Ericka sees her and smiles, Vicky smiling says, "I forgot you worked here."

"I 've been here a little over a year," she answers as they hug.

KJ, head nods what's up to her, tells his mom, "I'ma look around," as he walks away.

Reign looks at Vicky, "What brings you in today?"

Vicky happily responds, "I'm going to start working out and I need some outfits."

"That's great." As she shakes her head approvingly.

"Let's go over to women's sportswear. Are you going to be working out at home? Running around the block what's the plan?" They start walking with Ericka following behind.

"I just started a new job at my brother's workout place, and since I'm there I might as well get back into shape."

"What do you have in mind?"

They stop at the women's leggings that are hanging up on a circular clothes rack. Vicky's looking at different colors and styles not seeing anything that she likes. She mumbles, "I don't know if I am ready for these tight-fitting leggings yet."

Ericka and Reign are on a different rack looking at some joggers, Reign, "We have some joggers over here, they are not as tight-fitting, Vicky walks over, Ericka pulls off a pair of white joggers, "What about these?"

"Those are not my size, and I don't like white shows everything."

Reign looks at her and pulls out a pair of maroon joggers, "What about these?"

Vicky walks over and looks at them, "I like them and you even got the right size."

"After you been here so long you pick up that skill. Here is the matching top," she pulls a matching ¼ zip long sleeve shirt with the same colors.

She grabs another pair of blue joggers, "I'm going to try these on, as she walks away.

Reign and Ericka wait outside the dressing room, "How have you been doing Ericka?"

"I'm good…

KJ comes around the corner with a display store shoe, Where's momma?"

Ericka, "She's trying on some clothes."

Vicky hears this, "What's up?"

KJ, "I saw some shoes I like and I was wondering if I could get them?"

Vicky from inside the dressing room yells, "Give me a second I'm about to come out."

Ericka looks at the shoes, says "I want some shoes too."

Vicky yells from inside the room, "Everybody slow your roll."

She comes out and KJ holds the shoe out, it is a blue and white Giannis Immortality basketball shoe.

Vicky grabs it looks at it, "Nice shoe," she looks inside of it sees the price of $110. "I'm sorry honey I can't afford these."

He takes the shoe back, dejectedly responds, "Okay," and walks away.

She sees his disappointment, "If you find a pair for less than $100 we can get them," she looks at Ericka, "You too."

Ericka hears this, yells "Bet" as she shuffles to catch up to him.

After they leave Reign tells her, "I'll throw in my employee discount to help out."

"Thank you." She takes a deep breath, looks at Reign, "It hurts me to think about what could have been."

 Reign looks back, "We still family regardless."

"Last time we talked you were thinking about going to see DJ. Have you made a decision?"

"Yes, I gave it a lot of thought and my family thinks it might help with the healing."

"And KJ?"

"He's coming too but he ain't too happy about it."

She puts it out there. "My mind hasn't changed, I still hate him."

Vicky stops in the aisle, "Maybe you should reach out to DJ."

Reign looks at her, "I'm over it for the most part "pauses "I'm seeing someone new, and right now so far it's good. It's just when I think about Jordan is when it hurts So, I try not to think about it too much."

At the register, as everything is being rung up, and bagged, Vicky grabs a bag, then Ericka and KJ. They turn to walk out of the store, Reign grabs KJ, "Your mother told me y'all going to see DJ soon, can you tell him something for me."

26

VICKY'S CELL PHONE ALARM IS BEEPING, she reaches over to her nightstand grabs the phone looks at it six in the morning, puts it on snooze.

"Damn what have I got myself into?" She mumbles.

She lies there for a few more minutes drifting off, and then the alarm buzzes again.

She grabs the phone snoozes it again, texts Rodney, *Checking to make sure we're still on.*

She puts the phone back down and goes to the bathroom to get ready. The phone buzzes again while she is in the bathroom.

She comes out to turn it off and sees that Rodney's texted her back. *It's on!! I'm on my way right now. Let's git it!*

She mumbles, "Nobody should be that crunk this early in the morning."

She texts, Shea *You on your way?*

Dropping the phone on the bed she goes to the closet grabs the shopping bag from last night and pulls out the clothes and shoes.

She puts on the maroon workout pants and a gold t-shirt and the white and black Under Armour running shoes.

When the doorbell rings, she walks quickly to answer it because she doesn't want KJ and Ericka to wake up. She opens the door to let Shea in.

"Sorry I didn't answer your text I was already on my way here."

"The kids get up in about 30 minutes, they know what to do. They can eat some cereal for breakfast. They have to be at school before 830." She walks away to her room to get her matching zip-up top.

Shea walks in and takes a seat on the couch. She starts fiddling with Vicky's puzzle.

"Relax girl, I got this, Rodney is probably already there."

Vicky walks to the door, "Yeah girl I texted him and he was a little too pumped up for this time of the morning.

Shea laughingly replies, "Girl, you seen his body. That didn't happen by accident."

"Alright, wish me luck", she yells as she walks out the door.

Vicky pulls up and sees a big motorcycle in the parking lot.

She parks and thinks to herself, "This man is different, riding a motorcycle in this temperature is crazy."

When she walks in, Rodney is on the mat doing a standing long stretch.

She announces, "You must be crazy, riding a motorcycle in this cold weather."

He laughs, "I like riding in the morning. It gets the blood going and wakes me up. So, what we trying to do this morning?"

"You the trainer. You tell me," she snaps at him.

"What's your goal? What do you hope to accomplish?" How long do you plan to work out? I need your help if we are going to do this."

"I like how you keep saying we."

He smiles at her, "Well, we are here, together aren't we?"

She smiles back at him. He tells her, "Come on over here and we can start stretching."

She takes her jacket off and throws it on the Nordic track machine. He demonstrates the standing long stretch and tells her, "Follow my lead." They spread their legs apart and lean down attempting to touch the floor. While they're stretching he asks, "So what changed your mind?"

She looks at him, "What are you talking about?"

"Last time we were in here you let me know that you didn't want nothing to do with me. Yet here we are, what changed?"

He looks at her, "Well?"

"I had an unexpected change in my personal life and I could tell you were feeling me. After talking with Shea, I decided to take a chance."

"You are right I was digging you, but if you weren't feeling the same I wasn't going to push it. Next, do a hurdler's stretch." They get on the floor and bend their left leg behind and reach out to touch their toes with their hands.

After they finish stretching Vicky asks, "What's the plan?"

"Well since this is your first day we are going to get on the Nordic cycle and do some timed cardio. We'll take it easy the first few times to see how you adjust and take it from there."

"I haven't done any cardio in a minute so this should be interesting."

"You ready?"

She gets up off the floor and takes a seat on the cycle.

He goes over to the machine and starts programming it. She asks, "What are you going to be doing while I'm doing this?"

"I'm right here with you motivating you."

"That's just what I need a cheerleader."

He laughs and she laughs back as she starts pedaling.

After 20 exhausting minutes, on the Nordic cycle, the timer goes off. She practically falls off the machine sprawls on her stomach. She wails, "Damn that wore me out."

He leans over and asks, "You okay?"

She rolls over to her back and tells him, "Help me up" as she holds out her right hand.

He stands back up grabs her right hand and pulls her up. As she stands up she gets within inches of him.

She looks at him, and he steps back, "I'm sorry," she quickly says. "You just picked me up so fast it caught me off guard."

"I wasn't trying to do anything I just wanted to make sure everything is okay."

"Yeah I'm straight, my legs feel like rubber, I haven't felt like this since high school." She starts high stepping to stretch her legs

He goes over to the machine to check the display.

He yells to her, "You did just under two miles 1.7 miles to be exact."

He walks toward her, "That's great!!" he exclaims and holds up his hand for a high five.

Surprised by his excitement she does an awkward high five.

"We need to do a quick five-minute cool-down stretch.

He turns around to walk back to the mat to begin stretching when she grabs his hand and asks him, "Would you have a problem dating a coworker?"

Smiling at her, "You already know the answer to that." They embrace for a few seconds, he pulls back and looks intently at her. "You sure you ready for a relationship?"

She looks up at him questions, "Why do you ask?"

"The way you came off when we first met. I know something is going on in here." With his right index f nger, he points at her heart.

"I do have a lot going on and I have been hurt before, but Shea tells me you're a good man and thinks we should make a go of it."

"It's not about Shea. It's what you feel. We will take it slowly and see where it goes. Now let's get stretched and get out of here."

On the way to her car Vicky's phone buzzes it's a text from Omar, *"I'm going to visit Dejuan this Saturday.*

27

VICKY TEXTS BACK, *I will get back with you later today.*

She switches up and texts Shea, *How did it go with the kids?*

She gets to her car and gets in and backs out and heads to the street, Shea texts back, *Smooth sailing, np, how did the workout go?"*

Vicky pushes the phone button on the steering wheel to call Shea.

Shea picks up on the fifth ring, Vicky "I'm on the way home, it's easier if we talk."

"*I'm almost at work, so I won't be able to talk long. How was the workout?"*

"Well I'm exhausted he worked me good."

Shea laughs and replies, *"Girl I bet he did."*

Vicky laughs too, *"You know it wasn't even like that."*

"I'm messing with you. Well, what happened?"

"Girl nothing really, we stretched he put me on the bike and I rode for about 20 minutes."

"That's it? You were alone with him and all you did was exercise? That was the perfect time to talk to him."

"Well, we actually did talk after the workout."

Shea excitedly yells, *"I knew it!! You trying to be on the down-low, you must have forgotten who you talking to. I'm about to turn into the lot, get with me when you come in."*

"I'll see you in about an hour. Bye."

Vicky walks through the door and Shea is at the front counter talking with Rodney.

As she walks in she mumbles, "Look at her trying to pump him for some dirt."

They both immediately see her come in and smile and say "Good morning."

She smiles back and answers, "Good morning."

Shea tells Rodney, "Just get with me when he calls."

Vicky with a slight limp walks towards them he says, "Sore huh?"

She grimaces and answers, "Yeah a little."

He smiles and advises, "It will get better. Do you want to get lunch?"

"Sure." She gives him a big smile and limps to the office.

Shea catches up with her, "Slow down girl you know we need to talk."

They walk towards the office, "What did you talk about?"

"Look it wasn't nothing really too deep I asked him would he like to go out. He told me he could tell something was going on and that we could take it slow and see what happens."

Shea opens the office door and Antonio is working on the desktop. He looks up from the computer at Vicky demands, "Why didn't you tell me that Keith punked out."

They both walk into the office Shea goes to the other desk and starts logging on to the computer. Vicky stops between the two desks and leans on the desk Shea is working at. She looks at Antonio tells him, "Because I didn't want to have this conversation right here." She looks back at Shea and says accusingly, "I told you not to say anything."

Shea typing on the computer pretends like she didn't hear her.

He smirks at her and raises his voice, "I told you his punk ass would screw you over."

"I don't need to hear a lot of 'I told you so's. If that's where this is going save it."

"If you would have listened to me maybe…" Shea interrupts picks up his though, "Maybe this is a good thing. Now she doesn't have any reason not to give Rodney a chance."

She looks back at Shea, "It's not even about that I just wanted to give Keith a chance. Now that I see he is full of shit so I'm moving on."

"Well if I see him I'm going to set him straight."

Both Vicky and Shea look at him after that comment, Vicky responds, "Bro it's not that serious I'm good."

Antonio looks at her and says heatedly, "After the way he always fucks you over, you should want to get at him."

Both Vicky and Shea shake their heads, Shea mumbles, "Well I see where KJ gets his anger management issues from."

Vicky walks up to the counter where Rodney is sitting and talking with Rody.

She leans on the counter, "We still on for lunch?"

Rodney gets up from his seat, "Of course. I was just waiting on you."

Rody stands up half-jokingly asks, "Where we going?"

Rodney turns and looks at him, "Not today partner will catch you next time."

Rody looks at Vicky then turns and looks at Rodney, starts giggling and nodding his head, "Okay I see what's up. Alright, dog I'll get with you later."

He fist-bumps Rodney as he walks out from behind the counter.

Vicky turns and walks with Rodney out the front door.

Vicky, "I'm riding with you. Do you know where we're going?"

"What you feeling?" She smiles at him, "I don't know so surprise me."

They walk out to his dropped old-school metallic dark blue Ford F100 truck.

As they get in she replies, "I should have known this was you."

He gets in and starts it up, looks at her comments, "You do know that when we get back everybody going to be all up in our business."

She looks at him, "Well between Shea and Rody it wasn't going to be kept quiet for too long."

As he's driving down the road he glances at her, "Is that going to be a problem for you?"

"As long as you can keep work at work and personal things at home we good."

He looks at her shakes his head in agreement. As they drive Rodney spies a Substop coming up on the right, "Does Substop work for you?"

"Sure, that dude lost all that weight eating there. They must be doing something right."

He chuckles and replies, "You don't believe he lost all that weight just eating subs do you?"

She looks at him and shrugs as he turns into the Substop lot.

As they walk into the store, it is surprisingly empty. Rodney comments, "Looks like we beat the lunch crowd." They walk straight to the front display counter. A young lady comes up to the counter from the other side, asks, Vicky, "What kind of sandwich would you like today?"

She looks up at the menu, "Hmm, I think I'll take a footlong buffalo chicken."

Rodney surprised by her order exclaims, "Really?? You're going to waste our workout this morning by eating that. Didn't you just say something about that Substop dude losing all that weight?"

Vicky turns and gives him the evil eye. She sighs deeply, "Damn I hate when you make sense." She looks up at the menu again, shakes her head a little in an irritated tone, looks at the girl, "Give me a six-inch tuna on white." She looks back at Rodney snidely asks "Is that better?" Rodney a little unsettled about the attitude, "What you mad about?"

"Nothing I'll be at the table." She quickly walks away.

He looks back at the Substop worker shaking his head mumbles, "Women… I'll take a twelve-inch turkey club on spinach wrap with two large cups of water,"

After the order is finished he carries it over on a tray to the small table she is sitting at. He places it down in front of her and takes a seat across from her, "What was that all about?"

She looks at him as she is getting her sandwich off the tray, "I'm sorry, I'm just 'hangry' but you were right if I'm going to do this I need to do it the right way. Do you accept my apology?"

He looks at her smiles, "It's cool it's always tough making a lifestyle change, especially in the beginning. Trust me I won't lead you wrong."

She smiles back at him, "Ok Thank you!" She takes a bite of the sandwich. After chewing down the bite she asks, "What's your story?"

28

"WHAT DO YOU WANT TO KNOW?" He asks as he takes a bite of his sandwich.

"Everything, I want to know who you are."

He picks up his cup and takes a sip, "Let me see, I have four kids two boys and two girls. My oldest two are in the military. The third graduated two years ago and works at the factory, my youngest graduates from LBJ this year." He takes a bite of his sandwich.

She thinks to herself, *Jordan would have graduated this year.*

He continues, Two years ago Gabriella my wife passed away from a stroke. It happened so suddenly. We met in high school, the typical jock cheerleader deal, she was a senior I was a junior. We went to the prom together, that night we hooked up for the first time, and she got pregnant. She was crushed she had plans to go to college. Her parents were really upset with her. She got a job while I did my senior year. Our first son Rashad was born that following February. Anyway, I graduated and joined the Army. Got orders for Germany straight from basic. During my two weeks pass, before leaving we decided to get married. I was in country about six months and she came over, with Rashad. We had our daughter Giselle about a year later before we left country. After we got stateside we thought we were done having kids. As Rashad and Giselle got older, Gabriella wanted to have another one, so we had our son Peyton and two years later we had Alexandra. I got a medical discharge for PTSD right after Alexandra was born. After I got out I got on with Andrews Construction, I was able to work my way up from driving an excavator to Safety Engineer. Everything was so good, Gabriella was going to college part-time to get her degree."

He takes a bite of his sandwich shakes his head a little as the memories start to come back. "It started as a normal day, I had to be at work at six Gabriella took care of all the home stuff. She didn't have anything special planned for the day, run errands, clean up around the house, do her online schooling. She was supposed to pick up Alexandra after school. She waited for about one hour then called her but there was no answer. She got a ride from a friend who was in the band. When she got home she found her mom dead on the kitchen floor, still in her bathrobe."

He takes a big gulp of water looks at Vicky, and takes a deep breath, "Do you know how it messes with a 15-year-old seeing her mother dead on the kitchen floor?"

"Poor baby," Vicky says quietly. "My son KJ went through a similar situation, he saw his brother shot in front of him, and that is still messing with him over a year later. So how is she doing today?"

"She's a lot better, between all her school activities and her faith she is okay. She has occasional moments of weakness, on the day of Gabby's death, or her mother's birthday but overall she's good."

There is the obvious question that has been eating at her since Rodney's been talking. She is just unsure if she should ask it or not. She decides to go ahead, "I hope you don't think that I am being rude, but how did she die?"

He looks at her, "They believe it was a stroke … an Embolic stroke. She had an undiagnosed heart disease that caused the stroke. If somebody had been home she probably would have survived. After her passing, I fell into a deep funk." As he says this she shakes her head in agreement.

"I would stay up late drinking and missed work for days at a time. They told me to take as much time as I needed, but I abused it. I didn't care, eventually, they fired me. I almost lost my house, if it wasn't for my kids helping me out I would have."

She takes the last bite of her sandwich, "So what pulled you out of it?"

He looks at her replies, "Two things my kids and my faith."

Vicky surprised, "Faith? Really?"

He takes a big bite of his sandwich, answers back emphatically "Yes! I grew up in the church, in the choir, was saved, and all that. I can't say if I was doing it because it was expected of me or if I truly felt the spirit. As I got older I drifted away and had some years that if you knew me you wouldn't believe that I had ever seen the inside of a church I was so shady. I don't know what Gabby saw in me."

She chuckles at this comment.

"Getting married and becoming a dad brought me back. I knew I wanted to raise my kids in the church just like I was."

"We were going to church as a family but it still didn't feel right. After she passed away and I was going through my funk it was Peyton and Alexandra that led me back to talk with my Pastor."

"Pastor A. Williams met with me weekly for one on one counseling. Then I started going to bible study, and it just expanded from there, joining the choir, becoming a deacon."

This past summer me and Alexandra went to Germany to visit Rashad and Giselle, they both took leave and we took a mini-tour of Europe. This really helped me, I got a chance to spend some time with my children and get away and reset. I came back refreshed, renewed, ready to get back to the real world. Six months ago, I saw your brother had an opening on Indeed so I applied. He took a chance on me which I am eternally grateful, and here we are. Your turn."

She picks up her phone from the table looks at it "We need to be getting back" as she is putting the sandwich trash on the tray.

He chuckles as she is getting up walking to the trash can, "Don't think this is going to get you out of it."

After they get into his truck and start driving on the way back, he looks at her jokes, "What are you waiting for? Talk."

She takes a deep breath, tells him, "I commend you for your recovery in getting on with your life after your wife's passing. I am still in this dark place. My youngest son KJ saw his older brother Jordan murdered about a year ago, ever since that night he has been filled with hate, to the point he was going to kill that boy's brother. I have my own struggles over it. Now I find out my son's killer wants us to come visit him in prison."

"Are you going?"   "I believe so, my doctor believes we need closure."

"We?"

"Yeah me and my son KJ."

"I agree with your doctor." He pauses for a moment in a calm voice states, 'Love prospers when fault is forgiven but dwelling on it separates close friends. 'Proverb 17,9."

As he is driving she quietly sits there thinking about what he just said after a minute she responds, "Are you saying that by us not forgiving this boy for killing my son, it's causing me and KJ to have problems?"

He replies, "I don't know everything going on, but I will say that until y'all find some peace there is always going to be an issue"

"I think you're right and that's why we're going to visit him. I'm just not sure KJ is ready to move on."

"When are you going to visit?"

"This Saturday."

He turns into the fitness center parking lot, parks the truck looks at her, "I tell you what. If the visitation doesn't go well, I will introduce him to my youth minister to counsel with him."

She smiles at him, "I guess you are inviting us to church?"

"Is that okay with you?"

She turns and kisses him on his right cheek, "I haven't been in a minute but as you said earlier, I need to raise my kids in the word." She opens the truck door.

Completely surprised by the move Rodney utters "I don't know where that came from,"

She is still smiling as she walks around the front, "Don't worry about it, soak in the moment, and enjoy it. Let's go we need to get back to work."

29

FRIDAY AFTERNOON KJ AND ERICKA

are home. Both are in the living room on their phones. Vicky pulls up in the driveway, Ericka jumps off the couch and runs to the door, Vicky half expecting this stand there as she opens the door. KJ looks at her and shakes his head.

Vicky smiling says, "That never gets old," and she bends down to hug her and walks into the house.

She sees KJ on the couch. As she walks to the kitchen she happily asks, "And how was your day son?"

He looks up from his phone, "Cool", he notices her happy demeanor, "Is everything ok?"

She is in the kitchen, getting a glass of water to take her pills answers, "Yes, why you ask?"

Ericka walks to the kitchen answers, "It's been a long time since you've been so happy, it's weird."

She walks into the living room with her glass of water and takes a seat on the couch and Ericka sits down beside her. "There are a couple of things I need to tell the both of you, she looks directly at KJ, "Mr. Russell texted me earlier today, he is going to visit his son tomorrow. You still want to do this?"

He stops texting on his phone, stares at it, "Not really but if you want me to I will."

"Good I was hoping you would say that, I'm going to text him now."

She grabs her phone and starts texting.

Ericka asks, "What else did you want to tell us?"

Without looking up she answers "Just give me a second."

She finishes puts the phone on the coffee table looks up, "How would y'all feel if I started to see someone?"

"You mean dating?" KJ asks.

Hesitantly she answers, "Well yeah date someone."

Ericka excitedly asks, "Who is it?"

Vicky looks at her, "He is someone I work with at the fitness center."

"Was it the person you went to work out with this morning?"

She smiles even more answers, "Yeah, so what do you think?"

Ericka excited by the news, "I just want you to be happy. When are we going to meet him? What's his name?'

"We made plans to go to church Sunday. His name is Rodney."

Her phone buzzes, she picks it up from the coffee table it's a text from Omar. *Good, the visitation is set up for twelve. I can pick y'all up a nine.*

She texts back, *Sounds like a plan.*

Looking back at KJ, "It's on he is picking us up tomorrow at nine." He doesn't respond.

She gets up, "I need to get with Shea and see if she can keep you for the night."

She walks into Ericka's room with her phone calls Shea, she answers

What's up?

"I need a favor, I know this is short notice, can Ericka stay overnight with you? Me and KJ are going down tomorrow to visit Dejuan."

"No problem, you know I got you."

"I know I just, had to make sure you didn't have any plans."

"Me and Ant going to be pricing some new equipment for the expansion she can hang with us."

"Great, I'm packing her an overnight bag and I'll drop her by in about 30 minutes."

"Alright don't worry about dinner we'll be going out as soon as the twins get home from school."

"See you in 30 Bye."

"Bye." Vicky hangs up.

Vicky yells to Ericka, "Come in here and pack a bag."

Ericka gets up and goes into her room dumps out her backpack and starts packing.

Vicky walks back into the living room where KJ is still on his phone. She sits down on the couch, "Do you want to ride to drop off Ericka?"

Ericka walks out with her backpack hanging off her left shoulder. He looks at her answers, "No I'm good, I'm going to hang with Dre."

Vicky gets up, "Okay, I can't say this enough please don't get in any trouble. I'll give you a ride."

"Cool," They both get up and everybody leaves.

30

OMAR LIMPS TO DEZERA'S room he is still sleeping, He yells from the door, "Get up and get ready."

Dezera doesn't move, He limps into the room and kicks the edge of the bed. Raising his voice, "Yo let's go."

Dez rolls over and sits up. He mumbles, "I don't want to go."

"Why not?"

"I got a bad feeling, there's going to be a lot of drama."

Omar sits down on the edge of the bed, "Don't you want to see your brother?"

"You know I do, I just don't know if I could deal with them going off on him about what happened. I'll go next time."

"Yeah, it might get a little heated today, I'm not sure how I'll deal with it either, but your brother insisted on talking to them."

He stands up, "I will talk with DJ to let him know why you didn't come. You know I'll be gone all day."

He lays back down, "I'll be hanging with Jackson."

Omar walks out of the room and shuts the door.

Vicky and KJ are both in the living room waiting for Omar. She is sitting on the couch working on a puzzle. KJ is spread out on the love seat dozing off. A vehicle pulls up into the driveway. The horn blows two times.

Vicky anxiously gets up and goes over to KJ to shake him awake. "He's here, get up we need to go."

KJ stands up stretches his arms above his head. She grabs his coat and gives it to him, "Thanks, mom."

"Make sure you got your school id." She tells him.

He pulls out his purple and gold school lanyard from underneath his shirt with his picture id dangling from it. He holds it up for her to see.

"Just making sure," she says as she grabs her phone and wallet and stuffs them in her right coat pocket. "Alright let's go."

They walk to the truck, Omar is listening to the radio and smoking a cigarette. Vicky opens the front passenger door and climbs in. KJ gets in the back directly behind her. Vicky notices that Dez is not there, she inquires, "Where is your son?"

He puts out the cigarette, responds, "He didn't feel too well this morning, I thought it was best he stay home."

He backs the truck out as Vicky replies, "Something is going around my brother was sick earlier in the week."

KJ lounging in the back seat thinks, *Cool I ain't missing him.*

Vicky buckles up, "How long is the trip?"

"Around two hours so get comfortable."

KJ has already plugged in his headphones into his cell and stretched out.

Vicky takes her phone out of her coat pocket begins texting Shea: *We are on the way I will let you know when we get there.*

She puts it back in her jacket pocket. "Do you mind if I catch some sleep while we're on the road?"

"It's cool. I'm used to my son Dez sleeping all the time on the way down.

She lets the seat back slightly and leans back with it, "If I'm not awake when we're thirty minutes out could you wake me I want to get KJ up to make sure we're ready."

"Will do." He pulls up the GPS on the truck console. "I hope you don't mind if I jam some old school, Prince's, "Diamond and Pearls," comes on.

Without opening her eye, "That's all I listen to today, I can't get into this stuff they play now."

He chuckles, "That's cause you old."

She chuckles also, "You and me both. Don't forget to wake me 30 minutes out."

"Chill woman I got you," as Diamond and Pearls plays in the background.

KJ wakes up in the backseat, sees his mom asleep leans forward, and taps her left shoulder.

"Mom! Mom! I need to pee."

She wakes up and sits up in the seat shakes her head to clear the cobwebs asks, "Are we there yet?"

Omar laughs and replies, "I thought the kid was supposed to ask that."

She dismissively waves her left hand at him as she straightens the seat, "Can we stop at a bathroom?"

"Yeah, I can fill up while we there."

Omar pulls into a Quik Stop gas station and parks by a pump. KJ quickly gets out and runs into the store. Both Vicky and Omar get out to stretch. He pulls out his credit card to pay at the pump. She walks to the store to check on KJ. She pulls out her phone to check her messages, Shea has texted her back, *Be strong.*

She texts, *Thanks, we're almost there I'll get back with you on the way home.* She puts her phone back in her pocket and walks into the store as KJ is walking out, he stops and follows her.

She asks him, "Do you want anything?"

"A mountain drop."

"Go ahead and get it and get me a bottle of water."

He walks to the cooler to get the items.

As they walk out, Omar is on the side of the store smoking.

He sees them and puts out the cigarette and limps up behind them.

They all get back in the truck. As Vicky's buckling in she asks, "How far out are we?"

Omar looks at the GPS screen, "The GPS says we got another 30 minutes."

"What's it going to be like? I have been to jails and juvy detention, but never a prison. What do we need to do?"

Omar turns the music down, "Since you've done a jail visitation before it's pretty much the same. You can't carry anything in with you besides your ID, that means cell phone, keys, money nothing. They will search us before they let us in. He looks over at her, "No worries about your outfit."

"I want to thank both y'all for coming seeing how y'all reacted when I first asked you I was sure that it wasn't going to happen. What changed your mind?"

Vicky answers, "A lot of things. Well, I talked with some close friends and family and they believe it will bring some closure to our life to hear what Dejuan has to say. I know you know what he wants to tell us, so what is it?"

"I don't know exactly how he's going to say it but I believe he needs to look at you to show you he is sorry for what happened."

KJ explodes from the back seat and yells "Sorry! Him being sorry ain't going to bring Jordan back!"

Both Omar and Vicky shocked by KJ's outburst, look back at him. Omar yells, "What the Hell!"

She yells, "Boy what's the matter with you?" We talked about this. Now control yourself!"

He sits in the backseat sulking. His head tilted down eyes rolled up and he's breathing heavily. She spies his earplugs sitting in his lap. She grabs them and hands them to him, "Put your headphones on to calm yourself. We can't be having no meltdowns like this once we get there."

He doesn't answer, he sticks his headphones back on.

Omar shakes his head mumbles, "Boy he reminds me of Dejuan at that age, and that's not a good thing."

Vicky a little offended by the comment responds, "He ain't Dejuan. Maybe it's best if we don't say nothing."

He doesn't answer he hits the volume button on the steering wheel to turn up the music.

Twenty minutes later they shoot past the highway sign *Wallace/Ware Prison Unit 10 miles.*

He announces, "We're about ten miles out before we get there, I want to tell you that Dejuan told me because of the special circumstances with our visitation, we are not going to have our visit in the normal visitation room."

"What does that mean?"

"He told me we are going to have the visitation in a private interview room in case things get intense."

"This is the only time I'm coming so it doesn't make me no difference."

He looks in the rearview mirror at KJ who is still listening to music on his headphone, KJ sees him looking at him so he pulls off his headphones.

"You heard what I told your mama about the rules right?"

He shakes his head yes. "You got your school ID?"

He zips down his coat and shows the ID.

"Cool that should work." His tone changes, "That little ten-year-old tantrum you just put on ain't going to play in there. Keep that shit in check. The hate you have towards my son I get, but prison is the wrong place to act a fool, so do what you need to do to get your head right, listen to music, deep breaths whatever it is I suggest you do it now cause we got about ten minutes left before we get there."

He mumbles, "Yeah okay my bad."

As they drive along KJ sees a sign on the road that reads, **Don't stop and pick up hitchhikers Prison nearby.**

He takes a deep breath feeling butterflies building in his stomach.

Another five minutes down the road he sees another sign that reads *Wallace/Ware Prison Unit 5 miles.*

As they continue driving down the two-lane stretch of road, on the left side they see a large green field about 600 yards away from the road. There's a twenty-five-foot high fence with concertina wire around the top of it. Inside the fence are multiple blue aluminum buildings, some single-story others two or three-stories-tall. The guard towers are the tallest buildings in the compound. You can see two towers in the front with two guards standing outside of them keeping watch. The other two towers are in the background.

Omar says loudly," Well there it is."

Vicky looks back at KJ and smiles weekly at him. She is trying to put on a good face, he smiles back.

He drives down the road for another 30 seconds then makes a left turn into a long road with a sign that reads **_Dick Ware Unit Texas Department of Criminal Justice._**

"We're about 15 minutes early," Omar says as he turns into the parking lot. He drives around trying to find a spot close to the main gate. As he is driving down the row he sees a White Chevrolet Impala backing up leaving, "Perfect timing. Not as close as I wanted but better than the spot I had last time."

He parks and opens the center console. He instructs, "Everybody empty your pockets."

Both Vicky and Omar get out of the truck, She grabs her cell phone checks it for messages, and throws it in the center. She takes her ID out of her wallet and throws the wallet in the console. Omar outside the truck takes a $50 bill from his wallet and his driver's license throws it in the console. He puts the money and ID in his pocket. KJ from the backseat throws in his phone and earplugs and gets out the truck.

Omar grabs a cigarette from the pack and takes his lighter out of his pocket, lights one up, and throws the lighter and pack in the truck before locking it up.

With the cigarette dangling from his mouth, "Go on ahead, I'm get this one in before we go inside."

Vicky looks at him, "Where? This our first time."

He points towards the building, "Just walk that way till you come to a gate, I'm right behind you."

Both Vicky and KJ shake their head and walk towards the building. They walk in the parking lot between the row of cars.

She asks "Are you good?"

"Yeah, I'm good."

She grabs his hand and stops him. They look intently at each other. She tells him "Thank you for coming, I know you don't want to be here and I can't blame you after what he did but we're here now." She pauses, "It doesn't matter what happens in there you are my son and I love you. Nothing you can do in there is going to change that." He smiles at her and nods his head slowly, "OK I'm good."

"Okay," she answers and they continue walking holding hands.

Omar is behind them limping along puffing on his cigarette.

They arrive at the front gate, there is a small speaker box to their left.

KJ looks back at him and mumbles, "Damn fat ass…. and he smokes."

Vicky hears the comment and nudges him in the back, she yells back, "C'mon let's go."

He limps along about 10 yards away, "What's the hurry? We got time."

KJ' leaning on the speaker box moves to the side when Omar approaches. He pushes the red button on the box, a beeping sound comes from the box. He leans in to get closer to the speaker when a man's voice yells, "Who you here to see?"

"My son Dejuan Russell."

"Who is with you?"

"They're ummm guest, Vicky Skyy, and the boy is KJ same last name it's her son. They should be on the visitation list."

"Stand by."

After a two-minute wait, the voice tells them "You can come on up." Omar walks first with Vicky behind him followed by KJ. There is a click at the gate and Omar pulls it open and they all walk through. Ten yards from the gate are some glass sliding doors where a female CO is waiting for them.

She asks, "Omar?"

"Yes,"

"Let's go," she then walks into the lobby to where six people are sitting down. She goes behind the counter and starts typing on the computer.

Omar's standing at the counter, with Vicky and KJ to his left. She looks at Omar and asks, "Can I get your ID?"

"I've been here several times for visitation I should be in your system."

"I understand but I need to scan it to register your visitation."

He hands it to her and she takes the scanner gun and runs it across the back of his license. After he gets his license back he goes and sits down in one of the lobby chairs.

She looks at Vicky and asks, "This your first time?"

"Yes," she replies as she reaches in her pocket to get her license, "KJ show her your school ID."

He unzips his coat and takes off his ID and gives it to the CO.

She gets Vicky's license and starts typing on the computer. While she is typing, "There are rules that you and your son need to read before visitation." She stops typing and grabs two pieces of paper from underneath the counter and slides them to Vicky.

She continues talking, "Sign at the bottom once you finish reading."

She is now writing down KJ's information.

Vicky inquires, "Can I get a pen?"

She slides Vicky a pen, KJ snatches it and signs the paper.

"Boy you know you didn't read that," she tells him.

"Who cares? This is the only time we'll ever be here."

She grabs the pen and signs her paper.

The CO finishes typing on the computer and gives them both their IDs back, she walks from behind the computer, "Follow me."

Vicky follows behind her with KJ, Omar gets up and falls in behind KJ, "Where are we going?"

She walks to the rear of the lobby, behind all the chairs, there is a gray door with a black card reader on the right. There is a male CO and another man dressed in a blue suit standing by the door.

She walks up to the door with them following her, she tells the CO. "This is the visitation that is supposed to take place in the interview room."

She turns around and starts to walk away, when the CO asks, "Can you wand her before you go?"

She turns back around; the CO has the black metal detector wand out for her to grab.

She takes it and tells Vicky, "Step over here," as she motions with the wand in her right hand for her to come closer.

Vicky walks towards her, "Stop! Spread your arms and spread your feet shoulder-width apart."

She follows her instruction, "I need you to open your coat." Vicky zips down the jacket and spreads her arms and legs back out.

She takes the detector and starts from the right s de of Vicky's head works it down her arm to her side. Then runs it past her coat pocket down the outside of her leg. Then to the inside of her leg then finally down her left leg.

She moves it to the outside of the leg, up the rest of the body, and finishes up.

Vicky, "Am I good?"

"Yes." She gives the wand back to the male CO and walks away.

He takes the wand back, looks at Omar, "You ready?"

"Go ahead." He wands him then KJ, no problems with either one.

After it is completed he steps back and goes into the room. The man in the blue suit steps forward. "Good morning my name is Anthony Johns and I'm a courselor here and I have been working with Dejuan for the past three months. Due to the unusual circumstances of this visitation, we will be holding it here in the interview room.

Does anyone have a problem with me sitting in on the visitation?"

Omar asks, "Why do you need to sit in?"

"Think of me as an impartial mediator."

They each look at each other, finally Omar answers, "Whatever."

"Well since there are no objections, I guess we can get it going." He pulls on his ID badge on his belt clip and places it over the reader. The light turns green and he opens the door.

Inside the room, is painted gray, there is a solitary square table with four chairs around it. On the far corner of the ceiling is a video camera. Two CO's are standing on either side of the door. Sitting in the chair close to the other door is Dejuan.

Omar yells, "DJ!" he limps over to him as Dejuan stands up and they hug for 10 seconds.

"How you doing son?" Omar asks.

"I'm good. Just another day locked up wasting away."

Mr. Johns to Vicky and KJ, "Come in and take a seat."

KJ replies in a low voice, "I'm good I'll just stand right here."

Vicky goes and takes a seat directly across from him, while Mr. Johns sits to the left beside DJ.

Mr. Johns "I don't need to introduce anyone. So, who wants to start?"

Vicky looks Dejuan in his face says, "Before anybody says anything, there is something I need to do."

She leans over the table towards Dejuan and with her right hand slaps him across his left cheek. "That's for Jordan!"

She immediately sits back down; the guard is walking towards the table.

Mr. Johns puts his hand up to signal him to stop, "Everybody relax we knew there was going to be some intense moments."

She leans forward and smacks him again, "And that's for KJ!"

The CO walks over to the table points at her with a stern voice tells her, "That's the last time that's going to happen. Next time you will be kicked out."

Dejuan stunned by what just happened sits there his fist tightly clenched trying to maintain his temper.

Omar looking at Vicky yells, "You're not going to continue to slap my son and get away with it."

KJ leaning against the wall smiles. Vicky raises both her hands off the table to show that she's finished, "I'm done I promise I had to do that."

Dejuan with his head down looking at the table, fist still clenched, looks up takes a deep breath, looks at Vicky, "I understand, I told myself to be prepared for anything. He takes a deep breath continues, I would like to say I appreciate you and KJ for showing up."

Vicky looks at him with a slight scowl on her face, "I just need to ask, why did you kill him?"

Dejuan looks at her shakes his head back and forth, then drops his head slightly, and looks away from her, "I don't know. When he showed up that night at Reign's house I was startled I didn't even know he was home. Then he started popping off at the mouth. He pushed me on the ground and ran, and I just lost it and chased him. The next thing I knew I was shooting and he was lying on the ground."

Vicky with tears welling up in her eyes, "He had just graduated from boot camp earlier that day and you killed him and you don't even know why." She shakes and drops her head down struggling not to cry, "You killed Jordan when the whole world was his for the taking. You took something from me and my family that can never be replaced. Nothing you can say today can take away that pain, but you wanted to talk to us so here we are what do you want to say?

"I'm sorry for what I did. There isn't a day that goes by that I don't think about it. It's been haunting me ever since, pauses, I know nothing I say today will bring Jordan back, but I want you both to know that I am truly sorry from the bottom of my heart and I regret that it ever happened. Can y'all forgive me?"

She looks back at him her eyes red from the tears, "As a mother, I can't help but feel sorry for you. You are too young to be in here. What are you 17, 18?"

"18."

"I want to hate you, her voice drops in tone, I mean I really want to hate but I can't. All I see is a lost child who foolishly threw his life away the night he killed my son. She looks at Mr. Johns, "My Dr. told me coming here might help me find closure to bring peace to my life. She looks back at Dejuan with tears, rolling down her face reaches out and touches her right hand to his left on the table, says quietly, "I forgive you."

Mr. Johns looks over at KJ who is violently shaking his head no, he can't believe what his mother just did.

Mr. Johns to KJ, "Would you like to say something?"

He angrily yells, "I will never forgive you! You killed Jordan for no reason and were gonna kill me! I will never forget it!"

Mr. Johns stands up to offer his seat, "Would you like to have a seat?"

"I don't want to sit down! He looks at Dejuan screams, "I hate you, and Reign hates you. She wanted me to tell you she hopes you never get out and that you rot in hell when you die."

Dejuan is about to stand up, Mr. Johns puts his hand on his left shoulder to stop him. Dejuan in a calm voice answers, "Reign….. I used to blame her for the reason I'm here…. if she would have just given me another chance. This wouldn't never happened. All I can do is apologize for trying to shoot you, I'm sorry."

He angrily responds, "Bruh, I don't give a fuck about no apology! I wanted to kill you! I know I can't cause I made a promise to Jordan before he died. Then I ran into that fool Dezera and I found out he was your brother and I wanted you to feel how I feel right now. The gun I was going to kill Dez with I got from your boy Tristan," DJ hears this and his eyes widen, "He told me it was the one you used to kill Jordan."

Vicky hears this and her mouth drops open in shock.

He continues "I didn't know it at the time." A smile forms on his face, "It would have been so lit to pop Dez with the same piece you killed Jordan with."

Dejuan sitting there lets the words sink in. He looks down at the table and closes his eyes. He then opens them and slowly looks back up speaks in a low calm tone, "I'm glad it didn't come to that, hearing you say that takes me back to my old ways, and the result was your mother was going to be attending another funeral."

Vicky hearing this springs out of her chair slams her hands on the table and leans in towards Dejuan yells, "You threatening my son!"

Both CO's, rush over to the table and put her back in the chair, the lead CO, "Okay I warned you visitation's over, looks over at Dejuan, tells the other CO, "Take him back to his cell."

Mr. Johns looks at Vicky, "Can you please stop, control your behavior. How do you expect your son to mind if he sees you acting like this?"

Sitting down she shakes her head in agreement, You right, I'm good, I swear that's the last time."

Mr. Johns looks at the CO inquires, "Can we have one more chance? There are still some things that need to be addressed."

He doesn't answer he just walks back to his post at the door.

Dejuan turns and looks at KJ, "Do you think killing Dez would make you happy?"

I don't know but him dying by the same gun that killed Jordan would have been………. poetic payback. I just want you to hurt like I'm hurting. I can't kill you but hopefully, your life is miserable for the rest of the time you're locked up."

Mr. Johns looks back at KJ and tells him, "Dejuan is locked up but you are the one in prison with that mindset."

"I don't care, I don't have anything else to say." He turns and faces the wall.

"KJ!" Vicky yells. He doesn't respond he continues staring at the wall.

Mr. Johns, reaches out and touches her arm and shakes his head no

In a somber tone, he states, "Sometimes you dor't get closure. You just move on."

THE END

The complete trilogy. The order is **The Last Time, You Never Said Goodbye,** and **Closure. You can email me at** evwill64@yahoo.com for books **or Facebook DM me** for autographed copies. They are also at **105 Publishing and Amazon.**

ACKNOWLEDGMENTS

The trilogy is complete. This has been an incredible journey with these characters. The first book **You Never Said Goodbye** was meant to be a single story about KJ Skyy a troubled 14-year-old who saw his brother killed and his need for revenge or being able to find forgiveness. In **The Last Time**, I knew I had to tell Jordan's story. It was the driving force for the plot of **You Never Said Goodbye**. The ending had an unplanned cliffhanger that I had to address in **Closure**. **Closure** is exactly what the title implies closure for these characters. This is a bittersweet situation, I am excited about the opportunity to end this story and write new books with new characters. On the flip side, I have grown accustomed to KJ, Vicky, Jordan, Ericka, Reign Zooey, even Tristan, Dezera, and Dejuan, a part of me will miss them. I know some readers might not appreciate how I chose to end the book. I wanted to be true to the characters I did not want to adjust KJ's personality for a happy ending. This is the final book at this time, but who knows, I might revisit them in the future, I would be very interested to see how Ericka turns out maybe 10 years in the future to see how all these events affected her. I would like to thank the following people for making **Closure** possible. In no certain order.

Giving all praise and honor to the **Lord and Savior Jesus Christ,** I am living proof that through him anything is possible.

Choctaw Casino and Resort, Thank you to all my fellow associates who bought either book, there are too many to name. However, there are a special few who I need to highlight **Lanee Carter,** I appreciate your support and your feedback. **Ashley Cumpton,** while talking with her about this book she gave me the idea that became the cover. **Tracy Orr** who became my unofficial promoter of the books, I appreciate you spreading the word.

Karen Lowe, my editor, and proofreader, Thank you for finding the time to do this for me, I know you have other interest that you are pursuing. Two books down hopefully many more in the future.

My ATL cousins, **Marsha Roebuck-Smith and Pam Roebuck,** Thanks to both of you for your advice. I also would like to give an extra thanks to **Marsha** for taking the time to read a few early chapters to give me some additional insight.

Jason Raynor and Trish Jones of 105 Publishing, Jason I remember discussing this book cover with you and you said I was "family." At the time I assumed you said it to be cordial, I was wrong you have truly treated me like "family." Trish, I know I put you through some changes with this book cover, I wasn't trying to be difficult I just needed to feel it and I feel this cover. Any future books I write will definitely be with my "family" at **105 Publishing.**

Gayla my wife, gives me the space to do my thing and is also there when I need to bounce ideas off of her. A special thanks to you for the last minute editing. Thank you for believing in me.

You can reach out to me on **Facebook** with your thoughts and comments.

Please leave a review on **Amazon, Facebook, Twitter, Instagram**. Any review is very helpful. Sharing is caring.

This isn't **The Last Time** you will hear from me because I **Never Said Goodbye** and this is not **Closure.**

Made in the USA
Columbia, SC
05 June 2022